"And we *will* marry, Saskia. For the baby's sake. I can assure you of that."

The worst of it was that she had to bite her tongue not to simply agree to that, too. Even if Malachi was doing it for the wrong reasons, part of her couldn't help but feel it was the right solution for her.

At least she would have him in her life. And after the last few days, she was beginning to find it harder and harder to envisage a future with her baby without Malachi closely entwined in it.

"We'll see," she managed instead, acutely aware that this time it wasn't an outright refusal.

His eyes held hers and, try as she might, she couldn't seem to drag her gaze away. They stayed like that for longer than she could tell, an eternity perhaps, until they heard the consultant returning and he finally dropped his hands.

She felt the loss acutely.

Dear Reader,

Having written Anouk and Sol's story, Saskia and Malachi were waiting patiently for me to tell theirs.

I can still remember the moment that, without warning, the Gunn brothers burst into my head. Malachi, the serious, responsible older brother who had become a carer for both his mother and little brother at such a young age; and Solomon, the younger of the Gunn boys who had carried the weight of his brother's expectations.

Becoming a young carer for not only his mother but also his baby brother had made this hero determined never to be responsible for anyone again, though I knew from the start that he had the biggest, most loyal heart. He just needed the perfect heroine to help him unlock it—and Saskia was everything I could have hoped for.

Bright, passionate, fun—I loved her from the start. Even better, she had a way of getting under Malachi's skin in ways I hadn't even imagined!

I really do hope you enjoy reading their story as much as I enjoyed writing it.

It's wonderful hearing from readers, so I'd love it if you dropped by my website at charlotte-hawkes.com, or met me on Twitter @CHawkesUK.

Charlotte xx

SURPRISE BABY FOR THE BILLIONAIRE

CHARLOTTE HAWKES

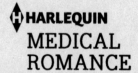

HARLEQUIN

MEDICAL
ROMANCE

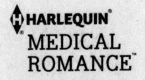

HARLEQUIN®
MEDICAL
ROMANCE™

Recycling programs
for this product may
not exist in your area.

ISBN-13: 978-1-335-14922-0

Surprise Baby for the Billionaire

This edition published by arrangement with Harlequin Books S.A.

For questions and comments about the quality of this book,
please contact us at CustomerService@Harlequin.com.

Harlequin Enterprises ULC
22 Adelaide St. West, 40th Floor
Toronto, Ontario M5H 4E3, Canada
www.Harlequin.com

Printed in U.S.A.

Books by Charlotte Hawkes

Harlequin Medical Romance

Hot Army Docs

Encounter with a Commanding Officer
Tempted by Dr. Off-Limits

The Army Doc's Secret Wife
The Surgeon's Baby Surprise
A Bride to Redeem Him
The Surgeon's One-Night Baby
Christmas with Her Bodyguard
A Surgeon for the Single Mom
The Army Doc's Baby Secret
Unwrapping the Neurosurgeon's Heart

Visit the Author Profile page
at Harlequin.com for more titles.

To my boys,

Even as I write this dedication, you are running up and down the decking, arguing over who has had a pop-up ice cream and who has only had an ice pop.

But I hang on to every moment of it because I can't stop time and it won't last forever; at seven and five years old, you are both growing up far too fast!

xox   I love you   xox

**Praise for
Charlotte Hawkes**

"What an interesting, fast-paced, surprising and entertaining read Ms. Hawkes takes readers on with this book...the dialogue was riveting and had me liking how these two interact; and everything this couple go through on their journey to happy ever after made this story fast-paced."

—*Harlequin Junkie*
on *Christmas with Her Bodyguard*

CHAPTER ONE

SHE COULDN'T HIDE away in here for ever.

Forcing herself to open her eyes, Saskia glanced gingerly around the stark, pristine hospital bathroom, relieved to find it was no longer spinning. She'd spent more time in one of these than she cared to remember over the past three months, but for once she wasn't here experiencing morning, afternoon, and evening sickness.

No, this time she'd ducked in here because she'd caught a glimpse of Malachi Gunn—looking as solid, as indomitable, and as smouldering as ever—stepping out of the stairwell to her paediatric ward. Apparently her body's fight-or-flight response had got its wires crossed and so she—the girl who was renowned for her fearless attitude and for never backing away from anything—had made a dash for the relative safety of the nearest ladies' room.

Not that it did any good, of course; in the end she was going to have to tell him. She had to, no matter how terrifying the idea of doing so might be. Besides, she *wanted* to tell him; she'd wanted to for the last few months. Desperately. She'd just been too afraid, and had no idea exactly what to say.

Because, really, how on earth was she to tell the only one-night stand she'd ever had in her entire life that he was the father of her unborn child?

In truth, she had been prepared to tell him both times she'd made her monthly pro bono visit to Care to Play, the centre he had set up where young carers could forget their responsibilities and burdens and simply be kids, if only for a few hours each week. But Malachi hadn't been there since their weekend together, which in itself had set off alarm bells in her head.

Admittedly she hadn't been coming to the centre for long—and only once or twice each month, and only since her engagement to Andy had unravelled so spectacularly—but as far as she'd been able to tell Malachi was *always* there, and the kids loved him. And they weren't the only ones—it hadn't been long before she'd started counting down the days to her next visit.

The fact that since their one-weekend stand he hadn't once been at the centre at the same time she had could surely mean only one thing—he'd been deliberately avoiding her.

It hurt more than she cared to admit.

Even now her hand went subconsciously to

her belly, where the tiniest bump was just beginning to make itself known. As though the gesture could somehow protect her precious cargo from the idea that Malachi wouldn't want to know. And from other people who might judge her or cast aspersions.

It shouldn't matter, of course. Saskia knew that. But you didn't grow up the daughter of a Tinseltown starlet without having people judging your every move. And she'd never really had as thick a skin as she'd pretended.

Not that anyone else could even tell that she was pregnant, of course. Not even Anouk, who had been Saskia's best friend since kindergarten and hanging out on a movie set where their rival Hollywood actress mothers had battled to out-diva each other.

Saskia felt a fresh pang of guilt about keeping silent with the one person she had always trusted most in the world, but somehow it seemed wrong to tell other people before Malachi. It was ludicrous, really, since she wasn't even sure he would want to know.

Besides, work had been so busy lately, and she'd already brought enough drama into her quiet friend's life by landing on Anouk's doorstep, suitcases at her feet, after she'd walked out on Andy.

Not that Anouk had ever uttered a word of complaint, of course. No, her friend had merely hugged her and then gone out and found a stunning two-bedroom apartment more suitable for them to share. Anouk had simply made it feel like an exciting new stage in the adventure on which they'd embarked over a decade earlier, when they'd boarded a plane out of the States in order to go to medical school in the UK and track down the father Anouk had never known.

It was bizarre, the way people always seemed to consider her to be dynamic and fun whilst they viewed Anouk as reserved, even a little cold. To Saskia, Anouk was focused, loyal, gentle—all the qualities that Saskia, who hated the way she herself seemed continually to find herself in the middle of some new, unwanted drama, envied most.

Gripping the moulded plastic sink top as she glowered at herself in the mirror, Saskia berated herself. *Anouk* wouldn't be hiding out in a bathroom on the paediatric floor whilst she worked out what the heck to say to Malachi out there. Then again, wise, pragmatic Anouk would never be pregnant from a one-night stand in the first place.

'Well,' she grumbled at her reflection, '*you* are. So you're just going to have to face the man and get on with it.'

With a satisfied nod, Saskia pushed herself off the cold plastic and marched across the bathroom floor. Then she hesitated. Carefully, slowly, she opened the door a crack.

And nearly fell backwards as a face loomed in the tiny gap.

'Oh, Saskia…' the voice cooed. 'You're not squirreling yourself away in the bathroom to avoid *me*, are you, babe?'

Gritting her teeth, Saskia opened the door firmly and forced herself to step outside. Babette was one of the paediatric nurses on Saskia's ward, and there was no way she could ever avoid the woman, however much she might want to.

'No, Babette, I am most certainly not trying to avoid you.'

Babette's laugh was more grating than tinkling, Saskia thought, and then chided herself for being so uncharitable.

'Are you sure? Only, I don't know how I'd get myself out of bed if I were you…'

Okay, maybe she wasn't being uncharitable after all.

'Indeed. But I'm lucky enough to have an ejector button built in under my mattress.'

'Really?'

Babette's eyes went large and round, and it was all Saskia could do to shake her head.

'No, Babette, not really. I was just joking.'

'Oh…' Babette narrowed her eyes in a calculating manner. 'Well, it's good that you still have a sense of humour. Especially now.'

Don't rise to the bait. Don't rise to the bait.

'What do you mean, "especially now"?' Saskia couldn't help herself, even as her skin prickled in warning.

'Oh, I *really* didn't want to be the one to have to tell you, babe...' Clearly the other woman could barely supress her glee. 'But I didn't want you to have to hear it from someone else. I feel... *responsible.*'

Yeah. Right.

'Tell me what?' Saskia managed, her heart now hammering around her chest so hard that it would surely leave bruises.

Lifting her hand, Babette waved it so close to Saskia's nose that she had to take a step back. But not before she'd noticed the huge, glistening stone.

'Andy and I are engaged.'

Her heart stopped in an instant. She was going to be sick. *Again.* She wanted to grab the wall behind her just to stop herself from plummeting to the cold vinyl floor, but she didn't want to give Babette the satisfaction.

Most days the shame of her ex-fiancé's betrayal didn't get to Saskia at all. But occasionally it felt as raw as it had ten months ago, when she'd walked in on him and his...mistress *in flagrante* in that on-call room, barely half an hour after she had been in bed with him herself in their own home.

Today was one of those raw days, Saskia thought with another sickening lurch—although, mercifully, this lurch was a little less intense. Not even when his new fiancée was standing opposite her and smiling superciliously.

'Isn't it stunning?' Babette cooed. 'Thank goodness! I was afraid he might get me something like a tiny quarter-carat thing that I'd need a magnifying glass to even see.'

'Perish the thought,' Saskia managed dryly.

Babette's eyes widened in feigned innocence.

'Oh, I didn't mean any offence about the ring he bought *you*, of course. I'm sure you must have been perfectly happy with it. I guess being the daughter of a Hollywood diva doesn't guarantee good taste.'

'Of course you don't mean any offence,' Saskia murmured quietly, ignoring the jibe.

She might have come to terms with her parents' death years ago, but it didn't mean she wanted someone like Babette dismissing it as though it meant nothing. Besides which, she was still fighting to quell the nausea as she thought of the tiny solitaire Andy had bought for her, on the premise that he was saving money for a decent house.

What a naïve idiot she'd been.

Then again, had she *really* been completely oblivious?

Sucking in a steadying breath, Saskia consid-

ered—not for the first time—whether she had
always known, on some level, that Andy was
wrong for her. He had been more interested in
using her name and perceived connections to
further his ambition of becoming a plastic surgeon to the stars.

Was that why, from the very first moment she
had stood on Anouk's doorstep, surrounded by
her worldly possessions, a strange tangle of emotions had tumbled inside her? Sorrow, humilia-
tion, and rage, of course. But then also fleeting
lightning bolts of something she had only been
able to categorise as...*relief.*

'Anyway, I just wanted to tell you personally. I
always pride myself on being honourable, babe.
And Andy agrees.'

Saskia's jaws ached from being clamped shut.
But it was better than saying that neither Babette
nor Andy would recognise honour if it danced
a jig in front of them. The woman would only
take it as jealousy, and Saskia couldn't bear for
Babette to think that. Or to acknowledge that
was her motivation.

*But that had been before Andy. And before
she'd fallen pregnant with Malachi Gunn's baby.*

How many times had she tortured herself over
the last couple of months by scouring the local
papers to see if there were any photos of local
events where Malachi might be seen with some
new, impossibly beautiful date on his arm?

Not that she'd seen any. But it didn't mean he was pining for her the way she seemed to be for him.

Saskia faltered, then caught herself. *No.* She'd be damned if catching her ex-fiancé cheating on her with the abominable Babette was going to change who she was deep down. Malachi was supposed to have been her rebound. Up until that night Andy had been the only man Saskia had slept with—*ever*—and Malachi was to have been her long overdue one-night stand.

Although if a one-night stand stretched into three glorious days and four nights of a long weekend could it still be called a one-night stand?

What was the etiquette?

Who knew?

Either way, despite the sick feeling she had now, the last thing Saskia felt was *jealous*. Certainly not of Babette or Andy, anyway.

But she really did feel ill. Another wave of nausea threatened to engulf her and Saskia pressed her hand to her stomach. The other woman didn't miss a trick.

'Oh, babe,' Babette crowed. 'I never expected you to take it this badly. I *told* Andy it was too soon. I hope it isn't going to be too much for you, seeing us together at the charity ball on Saturday night?'

Saskia fought it, but the darkness was closing in. Fast.

'It's not about you or Andy, Babette,' she muttered, as her mind fought to battle that little bit longer. 'I need you to get a doctor.'

'You don't need to pretend with me. I understand, babe. Perhaps it's better that you don't come...'

Through her blurring eyes Saskia could see that the woman was practically beside herself with joy at the idea that her engagement was causing Saskia such pain.

'No, Babette,' Saskia managed. 'You really don't understand. I need you to get a doctor. I'm pregnant.'

She just about heard Babette's shocked intake of breath as her head spun again.

And was that the floor coming up to meet her?

Abruptly, two strong hands grabbed her shoulders. Heat from a body was behind her back. An unmistakably citrusy, woodsy male scent filled her nostrils. And then she was being swept up into the oddly familiar arms of a hulk of a man, and nestled against his shoulder as he carried her down the corridor.

Malachi.

Her mind railed even as her body slumped against him, and by the time she came round fully they were in an on-call room and Malachi was sitting on the edge of the bed, cradling her head, a plastic cup of water in his other hand.

Saskia groaned inwardly.

'Stop squirming, *zvyozdochka*,' he commanded gruffly. 'You'll hit your head if you fall backwards.'

Reluctantly, she obeyed, taking another sip of the proffered water, then another, letting her mind stop whirling and twirling like the teacups ride at a theme park. As if water could somehow dampen all that heat and desire which she was sure still swirled around them even now.

At least he had the grace to stand up and move to the chair next to her, instead of being so close on the bed that it felt as though her entire left side was on fire.

It seemed like an age before she could shift position again, moving her legs to swing them carefully over the edge.

'Better?' he asked.

'Better.' She bobbed her head tentatively. Then, when it felt okay, she nodded a little more confidently. 'Thanks.'

But he didn't move. Neither of them did.

How much had he heard?

For several long moments a kind of tenseness swirled around them. Saskia waited for him to mention her pregnancy, but he didn't. Clearly he hadn't caught her last comment to Babette.

An odd sense of deflation rolled through her. She should probably be happy he hadn't overheard—that would have been no way for him to find out. But at least it would have taken the decision out of her hands; it would have meant she didn't have to sit here frantically trying to work out what to say and how to phrase it. Or even *when* to say it.

Her brain whirred. Whatever she said, though, dropping such a bombshell right now, in an on-call room during a busy shift, wasn't the way to do it. And that wasn't just an excuse. She *would* do it. Just not here, not now, and not like this.

'Anyway, I can't lie around here all day. I have patients to see,' Saskia began, forcing out an attempt at a jolly little laugh and placing her fists on the hard mattress to push herself to a standing position. Suddenly a tiny rod of hope punched through her. 'Although…you didn't come here to see me, did you?'

He didn't answer immediately, and it felt as though the air had suddenly been sucked from the room. Something dense and heavy was threatening to close over her, and before she could stop herself she began to babble.

'It's just…well, with not seeing you at Care to Play these last few months, I was beginning to wonder if you've been avoiding me. You know… after that weekend. What we did. Together.'

She tried for another jolly laugh, but it sounded as stilted and awkward as she felt.

Malachi hesitated. It was only the briefest of moments, but Saskia caught it nonetheless. Her heart launched itself at her ribs, slamming against her with painful force. It had been one thing to suspect it, but having it confirmed scraped at her much more deeply and painfully than it had any right to do.

And still she stood, rooted to the spot as he stared at her with a closed expression that said far more than any words could have.

The silence pressed on until she couldn't bear it any longer. 'I should go. Forget I said anything. I didn't intend to make things…'

'There's a patient called Izzy here.' His voice was clipped. Distant. 'She came in today after falling off a climbing frame. I just brought her mother in.'

Saskia snapped her head up.

'That's my patient.'

The seven-year-old girl had been brought into Resus several hours ago, where she'd been seen by Malachi's neurosurgeon brother, Sol, and Anouk, after she'd fallen from a rope climbing apparatus in the local park. Sol had told her that someone would be bringing Izzy's mother—who was an MS sufferer—in as soon as possible. She just hadn't realised that someone would be Malachi.

'So Izzy is a young carer from Care to Play? I didn't realise…' She faltered under the intensity of his gaze. 'I mean, I haven't seen her there before.'

'You haven't been going that long.'

'No…true. But Sol never told me it would be you bringing her mother in.'

'He has no reason to think you and I know each other.' Malachi shrugged.

He couldn't know how much that dismissive gesture cut her.

'How is Izzy, anyway?' he asked abruptly, his concern evident.

Saskia felt another stab of something she didn't care to identify. She forced it aside and made herself focus. In all her years as a doctor she'd never felt so torn before.

The young girl had landed on her face and her head and suffered loss of consciousness. Along with a laceration over one eye, and the loss of a couple of teeth, their main concern had been internal bleeds, so she'd been sent for a head and neck scan, with the possibility of a broken jaw. Fortunately the CT scan had come back as clear as they could have hoped, along with all the other tests they had run.

But she couldn't tell Malachi any of that. Not when he wasn't technically anything more than her patient's mum's lift in.

'I'm sorry, I can't discuss this with you,' she apologised. 'I need to speak to Izzy's mum.'

'Of course,' he confirmed instantly. 'I left Michelle with Sol before. She forgot some things in the car.'

For the first time Saskia noticed the small

pink rucksack Malachi was carrying. Despite everything she couldn't stop a little smile from playing at her lips; his evident concern for Izzy and her family was touching. Not that it surprised her. Malachi was as dedicated to his role as co-founder of Care to Play as he was to his multibillion-pound investment empire, MIG International.

The fact that he seemed so utterly committed to helping those kids had been part of what had attracted her in the first place. So different from her self-serving ex.

'I should go and see Izzy's mum. Bring her up to date.'

'Don't worry. Sol's with her.'

She tried to skirt past Malachi without looking pointed.

Not because she didn't want to touch him. More because if she did she was certain she would self-combust. Her mouth was insanely dry. Her body throbbed mercilessly. It was all she could do to keep her brain functioning.

'The little girl is my patient.'

'And Sol saw her, too,' he countered.

'I'm perfectly aware that your brother is a doctor. One of the top neurosurgeons in this place, in fact. But he isn't my patient's doctor now. *I* am. And, as such, I should be the one to talk to her mother.'

Saskia only realised she'd drifted forward

when her hands made contact with his unforgettable granite chest.

She leapt back like a scalded cat, and fought valiantly to drag her mind back to the present.

They'd had a gloriously wild, wanton time together, but she couldn't afford to rehash it in her mind. She had no claim on Malachi Gunn, and she still hadn't even told him her life-changing news.

And could she really drop her pregnancy bombshell on him? He had a right to know—but would he prefer not to? Her mind was spinning, and it didn't help that he was still standing there, scrutinising her.

'I really should go,' she said.

'I'd rather you rested a little more.' He frowned, looking irritated.

She shifted from one foot to the other, reaching out to place her hand on the door handle. But she didn't open the door and she didn't walk out. Instead she shuffled some more and wrinkled her nose.

'I'm fine.'

He didn't look impressed.

'Have you eaten?'

'I'm *fine*, Malachi,' she repeated, more firmly this time.

He lifted his arm past her, holding the door closed with his hand, and for a moment she thought he was going to say something else. Then, without warning, he dropped his arm.

She told herself she wasn't disappointed, yet it was all she could do to tug at the handle and make herself walk through the door, overcompensating a little by hustling fast to the unit where Izzy was being treated.

With every step she was conscious of the fact that Malachi was following her. It was all too easy to imagine his long, effortless stride as she schooled herself not to sashay her hips or appear in any way as though she was being provocative. No mean feat when her whole body was so hyper-aware of him, her belly clenching. If the baby had given a good, strong kick in response to Malachi's presence she doubted she would have been surprised, even though logically she knew it was far too soon for that.

It was as though the man was somehow imprinted on her. On both of them. She'd be glad when this moment was over and she could get away from him and back to her patients.

At least, that was what she told herself.

The truth was that she wasn't entirely convinced she was buying it.

CHAPTER TWO

WAS SASKIA PREGNANT?

Malachi sat on one of the plastic seats in the hospital corridor. Saskia was still in the room, telling Michelle about her daughter, and he was out here...uncharacteristically rattled.

His brain fought to focus; his body felt supercharged. He rolled the idea around his head as if testing it, seeing if it might fit.

Pregnant?

The problem was that he couldn't be sure. Certainly he *thought* that was the last thing she'd said to that godawful nurse with the irritating voice, but then he hadn't been thinking straight from the moment he'd stepped around that corner and caught sight of Saskia—the woman who had haunted his dreams for the last three months.

The blood roared through Malachi's ears.

And elsewhere, if he was being honest.

When he'd heard her mutter—*thought* he'd heard her mutter—that word *pregnant* as he'd approached, he hadn't really thought a lot about it. After all, she might have been talking about any one of her patients. Or colleagues. But then they'd sat in that on-call room together and she'd been so...*odd*...that slowly things had started slotting themselves into different places and suddenly he'd found himself wondering if she'd actually been talking about herself.

In that moment everything had...*shifted*. Kids. Family. Two things he'd thought could never be in his future. Two things he'd sworn never *would* be in his future. Not after the childhood he and Sol had endured. Not after becoming responsible and providing for his drug-addled mother and kid brother when he'd been a mere ten years old. He'd endured enough responsibility and commitment to last a lifetime, and he'd sworn to himself he would never put himself through any more as an adult.

Nor would he put any kid through the trauma of having someone as detached and emotionally damaged as he was for a father.

Instead he had dedicated himself to his work, his business, his charity. Partly because he lived for those things, but also because it ensured he'd never have time in his life for anything—or anyone—else.

And now this.

Maybe.

Possibly not.

Yet some sixth sense—the one he had trusted

his entire life, the one which had allowed his eight-year-old self to keep his brother and mother together and a roof over their heads, the one which had helped him make his first six-figure sum by the age of fifteen, his first million by the age of eighteen, the one which had ensured he could send his brother to medical school and make MIG International a global business—told him it was true.

No wonder his entire world was teetering so precariously on the edge of some black abyss.

How was it that in the blink of an eye everything he'd worked for could suddenly be hovering over some unknown precipice? Everything that made him…*him* gone in one word.

Pregnant.

His body went cold. His brain fought to process this new information and make some kind of sense out of it. But the only thing it could come up with was that any baby couldn't be his. They'd used protection.

He always used protection.

Except that first time, when all his usual rules had splintered and shattered one by one. Not least any thought to the notion of protection.

Which meant that he had no one else to blame for the fact that a baby wasn't wholly out of the question.

So how the hell was any kid to cope with him as a father?

Malachi's mind hurtled along like a car with no brakes. He was usually controlled, intuitive—effective when it came to dealing with business problems put in front of him—but right now he felt as if the ground beneath his feet was opening up. Instead of focusing on the issue all he could picture was her lush naked body, spread out before him like some kind of personal offering. He could still practically feel the heat from her mouth, as wild as it was sweet.

He couldn't say she'd been experienced, or skilled, and yet he'd never replayed sex with any other woman the way he'd replayed those nights with Saskia.

Why?

Maybe because he'd been lusting after her from the moment she'd walked into Care to Play as a medical liaison volunteer a few months earlier. Somehow during the so-called interview she'd ended up telling him about her failed engagement and her cheating fiancé, and she'd been so refreshingly open with him that he'd found himself captivated, wondering what kind of an idiot man would let a woman like Saskia slip through his fingers.

He'd had no intention of acting on the attraction, of course. Even as it had sizzled between them for months he'd been determined not to go there. Firstly, she was bound to be rebounding, and secondly she was a volunteer at the centre that he'd set up, and he'd told himself that was tantamount to making him her boss.

He'd even said those very words to her that evening at the nightclub, several months later, when Saskia, Sol, and a group of their Moorlands General colleagues had been letting loose for once, and she'd laughed in his face. Confident, sassy and oh-so-sexy, she'd told him in no uncertain terms that he was nothing like her boss. She'd also told him that maybe a rebound fling was exactly what she needed, given that she'd never had a one-night stand in her life before.

And he'd believed her. More than that, he had *wanted* to believe her. Because she'd spoken to something utterly primal deep within him…and what was the harm of a one-night stand?

Only he hadn't been able to let her go that night. Or the next night. Or the next.

It had been the most indulgent, incredible long weekend Malachi could ever have imagined, and when she'd finally left he hadn't been prepared for how quiet—how empty—his luxury bachelor pad would suddenly feel. As ridiculous as that was.

He'd fantasised about her returning with a sharpness that punctured him. Whether because he knew he was nothing more to Saskia than a rebound fling, or because he knew that he didn't have the time or inclination for a relationship, he couldn't be sure. Either way, what choice had he had other than to put a little distance between them and avoid Care to Play every single time he'd known she was due there, in the hope of letting that sharpness dull?

Only it hadn't dulled. It hadn't faded at all.

If anything, this latest encounter had only proved that he wanted Saskia more than ever—pregnant or not.

His baby.

It was enough to bring his head round a full three-sixty.

Surely he was the last person in the world who should ever have a kid? He wouldn't love it. That quality wasn't in him—not any more. It was gone. Spent. Used up all those years ago when he should have been the one being loved and cared for—not the other way around.

A baby?

He could provide for it, but he couldn't be the all-attentive father figure it would need.

Worse—and he was ashamed of this more than anything—he would end up resenting it, and the time and attention it demanded, the way he'd resented his own mother. The way he'd once resented even Sol.

He still hated himself for those feelings. Even now.

The responsibility he'd had for his younger brother since they'd been little kids had made him so angry back then. And even now, over two

and a half decades later, he still felt it. Especially
as Sol looked a million miles away now, a plastic cup of vending machine coffee in his hands.

'What's the story, *bratik*?'

Sol frowned before parroting out information
in a way that only confirmed that he was side-
stepping the real answer.

'The scan revealed no evidence of any bleed
on the brain, and Izzy didn't damage her neck or
break her jaw in the fall, which we suspected—
hence why she's been transferred to Paediatric
Intensive Care. Maxillofacial are on their way, to
deal with the teeth in Izzy's mouth that are still
loose. We have the two that came out in a plastic lunchbox someone gave to Izzy, but I think
they're baby teeth, so that shouldn't be too much
of an issue. We won't know for sure until some
of the swelling goes down.'

'I know all that. I was there when the paediatric doctor told Michelle.'

The paediatric doctor.

As though simply saying Saskia's name would
allow his brother to read the truth all over his
face.

As though he didn't know how every inch of
how her body felt and tasted.

As though she wasn't carrying his baby.

Possibly.

Probably?

Shaking it off, he tried for levity.

'I was asking what the story was with *you*, numbnuts.'

Not exactly his most convincing attempt at humour, but it was all he had in him. Fortunately Sol seemed too caught up in his own issues to pick up on it.

'Don't know what you're talking about,' he mumbled, a sure-fire giveaway that he was lying.

Malachi snorted. 'You know exactly what I mean. You forget I've practically raised you since we were kids. You can't fool me.'

Sol opened his mouth and Malachi waited for the usual witty comeback. But for once it didn't come. Instead his younger brother glowered into his coffee. Strangely, he was avoiding Malachi's stare. And when Sol spoke his voice was unusually quiet, his words coming out of the blue.

'I haven't forgotten anything. I remember everything you went through to raise us, Mal. I know you sold your soul to the devil just to get enough money to buy food for our bellies.'

The words—the previously unspoken gratitude—slid unexpectedly into Malachi's chest. Like a dagger heading straight to the heart and mercifully stopping just a hair's breadth short.

How was it that the very moment he was ready to doubt himself his brother seemed to say the words that made him think again? As if Sol had known just what to say when he couldn't possibly have guessed about Saskia being pregnant, let alone that it might be Malachi's.

Or was it just that he was reading into it what he wanted to read? Trying to convince himself that perhaps Saskia and her baby—*their* baby— wouldn't be better off without him?

Which made no sense—because he didn't *want* a family.

Did he?

Savagely, he tore his mind back to the present once more.

'Bit melodramatic, aren't you, *bratik*?' he gritted out. 'Is this about Izzy?'

'I guess.'

Sol was lying again, and Malachi couldn't say why he wasn't calling his kid brother out over it.

'Yeah. Well…no need to get soppy about it.'

'Right.'

Downing the last of the cold coffee and grimacing, Sol crushed the plastic cup and lobbed it into the bin across the hallway. The perfect drop shot.

Then, without warning, Sol spoke again.

'You ever wonder what might have happened if we'd had a different life? Not had a drug addict for a mother? Not had to take care of her and keep her away from her dealer every spare minute?'

It was as though the tiniest, lightest butterfly had landed on that invisible dagger in his chest, beaten its wings, and plunged the blade in that final hair's breadth deeper. Driving to the heart of the questions which had started circling around his brain ever since he'd heard Saskia utter those words to that nurse, creeping so slowly at first that he hadn't seen them over the chaos of the fear.

If he'd had a different childhood, would he be greeting this news differently now?

He didn't know. He never *could* know.

It wasn't worth his time or his headspace.

'No,' Malachi ground out, not sure if he was trying to convince Sol or himself. 'I don't. I don't ever think about it. It's in the past. Done. Gone.'

'What the hell kind of childhood was that for us?' Sol continued regardless. 'Our biggest concern should have been whether we wanted an Action Man or Starship LEGO for Christmas—not keeping her junkie dealer away from her.'

'Well, it wasn't. I wouldn't have asked if I'd known you were going to get maudlin on me.'

'You were *eight*, Mal. I was five.'

'I know how old we were,' Malachi growled, not sure whether he welcomed the reminder or not. 'What's got into you, Sol?'

Their shameful past—their horrendous childhoods—they were the reason why he'd always sworn to himself that he would never have a child. Whenever he looked back—which he never usually did—all he could feel was age-old bitterness and anger tainting his soul.

How could he ever be a good father?

Yet if Saskia's baby really was his—and he still needed to hear her say the words to him, not to some stranger—how could he turn his back on them?

He couldn't. It was that simple. And Sol raking up wretched memories wasn't helping.

'It's history.' Censure splintered from Malachi's mouth. 'Just leave it alone.'

'Right.'

His brother pressed his lips into a grim line and they each lapsed back into their respective silences.

He didn't want Sol's gratitude. He didn't deserve it. He hadn't taken care of their little family out of love, or a desire to be a unit. He'd done it because he'd been terrified of where they would all go if they were split up.

But he'd begrudged every moment of it. Resented the fact that at eight years old he'd had to effectively become a father to a five-year-old—had had no choice but to become the man of the house and earn money to put food on the table. At eight he had felt like a failure every time the electricity cut out and he had no money left to put anything on the card.

He'd sworn to himself that his adult life would be about himself, the way his childhood had never been. He'd been adamant that when he grew up he would never marry or have kids. His life would be his own. Finally. He had been determined that his business—which had made him a billionaire against all the odds—would be his only drive. As selfish as that might have sounded to anyone else—anyone who didn't know what his life had been like.

And it had been. Nothing had stood in his way. Not his lack of experience, nor the competition, nor any relationship.

He'd been ruthless.

All too often he wondered if the only reason he had founded Care to Play—the centre he'd set up with Sol, where young carers from the age of five to sixteen could just unwind and be kids instead of feeling responsible for a parent or a sibling—had been to make himself feel good about his ability to shake other people off so easily.

He'd believed that he wanted to make a positive difference to other kids' lives—if something like Care to Play had existed when he and Sol had been kids, then maybe it could have made a difference. He'd even convinced himself it was true.

But now, suddenly, he wondered if it had been just another selfish act on his part. If helping kids like Izzy, who clearly adored her genuinely struggling mother, was less about them and more about making himself feel better for the way he'd hated his own drug-addicted mother.

So now there was Saskia. Pregnant. With his child. And he couldn't shake the idea that he had to *do* something about it. He was going to be a father, and fathers weren't meant to be selfish. They were meant to be selfless.

Malachi was just about to open his mouth and confide in his brother, for possibly the first time in for ever, when Sol lurched abruptly to his feet, shoving his hands in his pockets the way he'd always done when his mind was racing, ever since he'd been a kid.

It was so painfully familiar that Malachi almost smiled. *Almost.*

'I'm going to check on some of my patients upstairs, then I'll be back to see Izzy.'

Malachi dipped his head in acknowledgement, but Sol didn't even bother to wait. He simply strode up the corridor and through the fire door onto the stairwell, leaving Malachi alone with unwelcome questions.

'You can go back in now.'

Malachi jerked his neck around, and the sight of Saskia standing there brought a thousand questions tumbling to his lips.

'Is there anything you'd like to tell me?' he rasped, before he could swallow the words back.

She blanched, her eyes widening for just a

fraction of a second before she pulled a smooth veneer into place.

'If you want to know about Izzy then you'll have to ask her mother. As you aren't a direct family member, it isn't my place to tell you.'

Was she playing a game? He couldn't tell.

'Tell me, do you always faint like that?'

Two high spots of colour suffused her cheeks. 'Of course not.'

'Then perhaps you'd like to explain what this morning's little episode was all about.'

For a moment he thought she looked panicked.

'That was a one-off.'

'Is that so?'

'It is.'

He arched his eyebrows. 'And why do you think this "one-off" episode happened?'

She shook her head back, straightening her shoulders. It shocked Malachi to realise that he knew her well enough to know it was a stalling tactic.

Or, more pertinently, it *should* have shocked him.

'I don't know,' she asserted. 'Like you said, I probably hadn't eaten properly, so I was running on empty. I didn't have a proper breakfast and it's been a long shift.'

He didn't know whether to be impressed or insulted that she lied so easily. Straight to his face. And then, without warning, anger surged through him—whether at the way she wanted to exclude him or at the fact she thought he was *that* blind, he couldn't be sure—but he quashed it, quickly and effectively.

Never let anyone see they can get to you.

Another life lesson he'd been forced to learn from an early age.

So this was the game she wished to play?

Well, he was just going to have to find a way to play against her.

Not here, not now. Not with Izzy injured in that room. Her mother and sister would need his support more than ever right now. They had no one else, which was what made the centre so vital.

Right now he was here for Michelle and her daughters. Saskia and her lies would have to wait.

But if that was her game, then fine; he would play her at it and he would win. He just needed to take a step back and regroup so he could work out his next move.

CHAPTER THREE

'THIS PLACE IS STUNNING...' Anouk breathed as she took in the huge sandstone arches reaching up as though in exultation to a breathtaking stone-carved vaulted ceiling.

'Isn't it?' Saskia demurred, following her friend's gaze, trying to quell the kaleidoscope of butterflies which seemed to have taken up residence in her stomach ever since Anouk had told her she had two tickets to a gala evening and asked Saskia to join her.

A gala evening for a local young carers' charity.

Saskia had known instantly whose charity it was. Anouk had mentioned something about Sol giving them to her, and something about a patient... Izzy? To her shame, Saskia hadn't really been listening—she'd been too caught up in her own head.

Tickets to a charity event for Care to Play. As though fate itself was intervening.

Saskia hadn't even asked how her friend had

got the tickets, or why. She just knew that Malachi would be there and that this was her chance to do what she should have done two months ago. She had to tell him about the baby. Whatever he chose to do after that was his business.

'I feel positively shabby by comparison.'

Anouk was still gazing at the architecture and Saskia laughed, grateful for the momentary distraction.

'Well, you don't look it,' she told her friend. 'You look like you're sparkling, and it isn't just the new dress. Although I'm glad you let me talk you into buying it.'

'I'm glad I let you talk me into buying it, too,' admitted Anouk, smoothing her hands over her dress as though she was nervous.

'You look totally Hollywood,' Saskia assured her wryly, knowing that it would break whatever tension her friend appeared to be feeling.

'Don't.' Anouk shuddered on cue. 'I think I've had enough of Hollywood to last me a lifetime.'

'Me, too.' More than anyone else could ever possibly know, thought Saskia. 'But still, the look is good.'

'Maybe I should be in a more festive colour.'

Anouk glanced at Saskia's own dress enviously—another much-needed boost to Saskia's uncharacteristically wavering confidence.

In fact, her friend had already waxed lyrical about the 'stunning' emerald dress, claiming that it might have looked gorgeous on the rack but 'on your voluptuously feminine body it looks entirely bespoke'.

For a moment Saskia had been worried that it had been code for, *I can tell you're pregnant and it's beginning to show.* Even though Saskia knew she wasn't showing at all. There wasn't a hint of any swell over her abdomen yet, and she couldn't help wondering if it was this lack of physical manifestation of her pregnancy which had stalled her in seeking Malachi out at MIG International when he hadn't shown up at Care to Play.

As if a part of her believed he might doubt what she was saying if he couldn't see it for himself.

'I think I look like a Christmas tree.' Saskia made herself laugh again, with a wave of her hand towards the glorious eighteen-foot work of art which dominated the entrance of the venue. 'Although if I looked *that* amazing I'd be happy.'

'You look even better and you know it.' Anouk replied instantly. 'You've only just walked in and you've turned a dozen heads.'

And yet there was only one head she wanted to turn. Supposed rebound or not.

'They're probably looking at you—and, either way, I don't care. Tonight, Anouk, we're going to relax and enjoy ourselves.'

'We are?'

'We are,' Saskia said firmly, hoping she was convincing her friend even if she wasn't convincing herself.

She snagged a champagne flute from the tray of a passing waiter, for something to do with her hands, before realising she couldn't drink it and passing it straight to Anouk. 'Starting with this.'

'You still feeling sick?' Anouk frowned, eying her with a little too much intensity.

'Yeah,' she lied, and another stab of guilt shot through her as she tried to suppress the heat flooding her cheeks.

Anouk didn't look convinced. If anything, her friend seemed to tense, as though she knew.

The guilt pressed in harder. They'd never deceived each other in over twenty-five years. As soon as she'd told Malachi she would tell Anouk. Why hadn't she told her before? Was it because she'd always known that, much as her best friend had never encouraged her to leave her ex-fiancé, Anouk had never really taken to Andy?

Ironically, Anouk had even apologised on the one occasion when Saskia had pressed her for an opinion, only for her friend to tell her that whenever she looked at Andy all she saw was another playboy—just like Anouk's mother's lovers.

'Relax.' Saskia nudged her gently now. 'Enjoy your drink.'

'I don't really like...' Anouk began, but her friend shushed her.

'You do tonight.'

Anouk balked, and Saskia knew that all Anouk could see was her mother, downing glasses of wine and popping pills.

'One glass doesn't make you your mother.' Saskia linked her arm through Anouk's, reading her mind.

It was Anouk's turn to offer a rueful smile. 'That obvious, huh?'

'Only to me. Now, come on, forget about your mother and enjoy this evening. You and I both deserve a bit of time off—and, anyway, we're supporting a good cause.'

'We are, aren't we?' Anouk nodded, dipping her head and taking a tentative sip.

Saskia told herself to stop scanning the room for Malachi, like some meerkat on watch duty. If it was meant to happen tonight, then it would. Otherwise she would go to his offices in the morning and she would finally tell him.

He had a right to know. And he had a right not to want to be involved.

She wouldn't force him.

He would have to want her. And their child.

'A word.'

Every inch of her skin prickled into goosebumps at the rich, deep sound of Malachi's voice in her ear. As lethally silky as the hand sliding around her elbow even now.

And something about the tone sent a warning whisper coiling its way through her body.

He couldn't know about the baby, could he?

Unless he'd spoken to Babette.

Saskia cursed inwardly. She was an idiot for letting that woman get to her enough to tell her a single thing, let alone for Babette to be the first person to find out that she was pregnant.

She couldn't shake the idea that Malachi knew and, worse, that he'd found out from her ex-fiancé's new fiancée instead of straight from her. It was little wonder that the air between them positively hummed with barely restrained tension.

Saskia wasn't sure why she allowed him to lead her across the ballroom at the charity gala without even a word of objection.

She'd only managed to slip away from Anouk by taking advantage of Sol's unexpected appearance to pretend she was going to check the seating plan. Just so that she could see if she could find Malachi.

And now he'd found her.

If he'd come to say what she feared then she had only herself to blame. She should have told him herself. The unspoken accusations already bombarding her were her own fault for being such a coward. And the longer the silence the more forcefully they hurtled into her, leaving her edgy and agitated and full of apprehension—and something else which she didn't care to examine too closely at all.

As if Malachi knew that the uncertainty was unsettling her, he seemed to be prolonging it, by not speaking another word until they were near the now deserted entrance, well away from the beautiful, well-heeled crowd bustling inside the ballroom, each jostling to set themselves ahead of the pack. Too many of them would be competing with each other to write the biggest cheques just to prove who was higher up the food chain.

It was disheartening to see just how few of them were actually there because they cared about the charity. About the kids.

Like Malachi does?

Abruptly Saskia pulled her head back to the present just as Malachi stopped, turning her to face him before he released her. The fierce, furious expression on his face was one she hadn't ever seen before, but she feared she could read it in an instant.

'It's mine.'

So that answered *that* question, at least.

Malachi knew she was pregnant, and whether Babette had told him, or someone else had, it hardly seemed to matter now.

Saskia fought to breathe. It was as though someone was sitting on her chest, squashing her lungs, stealing her air. Perhaps it was at the sight of the utterly masculine, foreboding figure in front of her. Or maybe it was because he was suddenly watching her with a cold, hostile expression in those eyes, when up until now she'd only ever known them to be kind and friendly—the colour of the richest, warmest cognac in his enviable drinks cabinet.

Every thought fell from her head, and everything tumbled around her. Her heart accelerated so fast she could barely even feel it. Or maybe it simply stopped.

And then suddenly a sense of calm overtook her and she knew she couldn't deny it. There was only one thing she could say.

'Yes.'

He tilted his head sharply.

'I suppose I should be grateful you didn't make this any more complicated than it already is by lying.'

Then, taking her elbow again, he steered her outside, neither of them speaking a word, and into the back of his waiting car. When he slid in beside her, filling up every last bit of space, Saskia was sure she was going to suffocate from the sheer pressure of the moment.

And all the heat she remembered from their time together—the heat which had been simmering again the other day at the hospital—flooded around her, almost drowning her in its intensity.

Lord, how was she to survive being in such proximity to him when a traitorous part of her wanted to revisit every inch of that hewn, addictive body which the tuxedo did nothing to temper?

'May I ask where we are going?' she asked primly, surprised at how even her voice sounded when she might have expected it to be shaking.

The unexpected truth was that it was almost a relief.

'My place.'

His tone was grim but he didn't even look at her. His gaze was trained out of the window, as if he couldn't bear to.

It hurt. More than it had any right to.

'Why?'

Her voice was sharper than she'd intended, but the idea of being back in his penthouse was daunting. Every room would surely trigger X-rated memories of their weekend together—and she already had enough of them in her own brain, without returning to the scene of the crime.

His head swivelled slowly to face her and abruptly she decided she preferred him staring out of the window after all.

'To discuss how we proceed from here.'

His low, controlled voice didn't fool Saskia for a second. And there was a carefully restrained fury in the cognac depths of his eyes—though whether that was because she was pregnant or because she had concealed it from him, she couldn't quite be certain.

Either way, he sounded ominous. Especially when she already knew what kind of a force of will Malachi Gunn was.

There was something else in those depths, too—and it was infinitely more dangerous than his anger.

Desire.

Still.

She could feel it rolling over her body as sure as if it were his hands themselves.

A low ache began building *right there*. Right between her legs, deep and insistent, and only Malachi had ever made her feel it.

Good grief, she couldn't trust herself around him for a moment.

The realisation was like a blow to the gut. If she went back to his apartment it would only amplify her haywire emotions that much more. Until they were completely out of control. Until *she* was.

Panic clutched at Saskia.

'Stop the car,' she muttered abruptly.

'Sorry?'

'I said, *stop the car*.' She raised her voice, tapping on the glass between them and the driver. 'I need some air.'

She was vaguely aware of Malachi dipping

his head in confirmation before the car slowed. Stopped.

Saskia was out in an instant—but not fast enough to beat Malachi, who had materialised right by her side. He took their coats from his driver, who must have retrieved them from the cloakroom before they'd left the gala.

Why was she even surprised? Of *course* Malachi hadn't left the event on a whim. The man never did anything on a whim. Except that long weekend with her, that was.

And now this baby.

Taking her arm, Malachi steered her to the riverside. The bracing air walloped her, mercifully knocking her out of her panic.

'Not exactly the balmiest evening for a walk along the promenade.' His tone was clipped. 'But at least the wind has dropped.'

'It's invigorating,' she lied, turning away from him and beginning to walk.

Anything was better than being pressed up to him within the confines of that car. Remembering the feel of his hands as they had explored every last millimetre of her body with such reverence. The heat from his breath as he had tracked down the column of her neck, leaving her shivering with desire and desperate for more. And the way he had moved between her legs, holding himself up and locking his eyes with hers before he surged into her, making her whole world explode in a riot of colours she'd never known before.

Had that first time been the moment the die had been cast? The moment her journey to pregnancy had begun? Or had that been later, in his apartment? On the couch or on the rug? In the swimming pool or in the bedroom? In his shower or in his bed?

He had claimed her over and over and over again, as if she were his.

She had actually felt like she was. For that one incredible weekend.

And then it had been over.

She'd made herself leave, sneaking out when he hadn't been able to postpone a conference call for a fourth time, because she'd been afraid she wouldn't be able to walk out through the door if he was watching her.

Over the last three months she'd told herself that she'd imagined the way it had been between them. That her memories had been blown out of proportion to all reality.

Now, with her body reacting in ways it had no business doing, Saskia was beginning to fear that her memories hadn't even done reality justice.

'Is this really where you want to talk?'

Malachi's rich voice cut through her thoughts. She toyed with telling him that a part of her didn't want to talk at all. But she knew that would be unwise. Either way, it was better here…where her body wasn't so assaulted by memories.

'There's no one around.' She shrugged, even as a faint shiver entered her voice.

She wouldn't last long in this cold, wearing only what she had on. He would use that to his advantage.

'So be it.'

They managed about fifty metres in silence, but if she'd been hoping the location might put him off then clearly she'd been mistaken.

'Were you planning on telling me?' he demanded, without preamble.

When she didn't answer it appeared that he couldn't stop himself from goading her—just a little.

'Or was there some doubt in your head that it was mine?'

She lifted her eyes up to his dark, blazing ones. A sense of belated dignity was apparently struggling to make itself known.

'*Is* yours.'

'Sorry?'

'Is,' she repeated clearly. 'Not *was.*'

'My apologies.' He didn't look in the slightest bit apologetic.

'And, for the record, I don't make a habit of one-night stands,' she managed stiffly, compelled to make the point even though it didn't remotely answer his actual question. 'I've slept with two people in my life. Andy was my first. You were my second.'

Another flash she couldn't recognise went through his eyes, and another thread of taut silence wove its way around them, as if binding them tighter together even in the expanse of the promenade.

'Is that so?'

She licked her lips.

'It is. And I know I told you that already. Three months ago.'

He still didn't answer, and she had to wonder whether her pedantry made her more of an idiot in his eyes or less. Either way, his intense glower did funny things to her insides. The way it had three months ago. And the way it had every time she'd thought of him since then.

Except that *this* was so much more…real. So much more potent.

'You should have told me,' he growled.

Yes, she should have. No matter how she ran events through her head, that simple fact was unmistakable.

Saskia paused. She wasn't used to feeling so cautious, as though she was on the back foot. She prided herself on being confident, strong and bold. Ordinarily she would have brazened it out. But then ordinarily she wouldn't have been facing off against Malachi.

Still, she tilted her head up boldly.

'I know that it was a one-night stand. I understand that. And that this is an unforeseen consequence. But I want to keep my baby, and that's
my choice. It doesn't have to be yours. Right
here, right now, I'm officially releasing you from
any responsibility.'

'Is that so?'

His eyes glittered furiously, and it was all
Saskia could do to hold her ground.

Not that she thought she was in any dan-
ger from Malachi—at least not physically. But
emotionally…? That was a whole different con-
cept.

It made her choose her next words very, very
carefully. 'I'm trying to be reasonable here,' she
offered at last, trying surreptitiously to take a
step back.

He took a step closer to her. Just one, single
step. But his stride was longer than hers anyway,
and it was enough to force her to tip her head
back to look up at him.

Enough for her entire traitorous body to leap
in thrilled anticipation. Her hands actually itched
to reach up and grab the material of his dark
wool coat which had no business clinging to
every ridge and muscle which she already knew
lay beneath.

'Reasonable?' he echoed quietly. Too quietly.
'Is that what you call it, *zvyozdochka*?'

'It is.'

Her voice was altogether too raspy for her own liking. And the name he'd called her that first night coursed through her as though it somehow made her his.

She took another step back before she realised how it might look to him. 'You don't agree?'

'Damned right I don't,' he growled, taking them both another step backwards, until she felt the cold sea wall against her back and realised she had no further to go, and his arms locked down either side of her, effectively to cage her.

What was wrong with her that she found the whole thing so utterly arousing?

He wasn't some knight, claiming her. And she certainly wasn't a damsel in distress.

'That's *my* baby you're carrying. You don't have the right to "release" me from it as though I have no say in the matter. As though the baby has no right to a father.'

'That wasn't…' She shook her head. 'That isn't what I'm doing.'

'That's exactly what you're doing.'

'No. I was just…' She took a breath, trying to get her thoughts straight in her head before attempting to articulate them. 'You said that I should have told you, and you're right—I should have. I was all geared up for it the first couple of times I went to Care to Play, only you weren't there.'

She stopped, giving him a chance to respond.

Almost hoping that he would say something to explain it, but he didn't. Yet his expression had altered and her heart tumbled.

She was right. He had been avoiding her.

'You were always there before we had that weekend together,' Saskia whispered, with no idea how she managed to stay upright, to seem confident, when inside she was crumbling like a sandcastle on the beach under the onslaught of the incoming tide. 'But after that weekend you were never there. At least not when you knew I would be. As though you were avoiding me...'

And still he didn't answer. He didn't even move. If she hadn't known better she might have thought he'd turned to stone.

She didn't want to hear the answer—she didn't *need* to hear it. She already knew the truth. Still, she couldn't stop the question from slipping off her lips.

'*Were* you avoiding me, Malachi? Were you so concerned that if I saw you at the centre again I'd take it as some sort of sign that we were in a relationship?'

CHAPTER FOUR

MALACHI COULD BARELY remember getting Saskia back into the car, or telling his driver to continue. His mind was too full of emotions so tightly entangled that he couldn't hope to begin to unravel them.

But suddenly he was tapping in the code to let them into his penthouse suite, and the moment Saskia stepped over the threshold he was assailed with images of the last time she'd been there.

He hadn't felt this out of control, this blindsided, since he'd been a kid.

It had been one thing to suspect that Saskia was pregnant, but quite another to actually hear her confirm it. His worst fear.

At least that was what he'd always thought it would be. That was why he'd always been so fastidious about using protection with all his other women.

Only now it wasn't fear he was feeling. It was guilt. Because Saskia was right—ever since their weekend together he *had* been avoiding her. Not because he was afraid, as she'd suggested, that if she saw him again she'd take it as some sign that he wanted more, but rather because a foolish, traitorous part of himself *did* want exactly that, and he was afraid she saw him as nothing more than a much-needed rebound. A fling to be dismissed and forgotten.

Which was why it made no sense at all.

He should have welcomed that—the lack of complication. He might not have the playboy reputation his brother did, but he'd had his fair share of women seeking a relationship with him when he could offer them nothing more than the physical.

Yet, as much as he'd kept telling himself that the weekend with Saskia had just been about sex, deep down he suspected there had been more to it than that. Some deeper, inexplicable connection had drawn him to her from the moment she'd walked into his centre and volunteered her skills as a paediatric doctor.

At a time when other people might have focused on themselves, on what they were personally going through—in Saskia's case, the breakdown of her engagement—Saskia's instinct had been to reach out and try to help others. It said more about the kind of person she was, about her generosity of spirit and her selflessness, than anything she could have told him.

Malachi busied himself trying to get his head

around this new, unwanted revelation. This wasn't the time for overanalysing what he did or didn't feel. Or for reading something into nothing. This was the time for taking a problem, looking at it logically and dispassionately, and finding the best response.

Something he usually excelled at.

But he was failing today.

'So, what now?' Saskia managed, in an impressive show of confidence.

Especially after the way she'd halted so abruptly, not allowing herself to progress much further into his apartment before she spun back to face him. And the way her eyes slid away from the room to focus on some point just over his left shoulder, where the front door now closed slickly behind him.

Almost, he considered, as if she couldn't bear to look at the room where he'd stripped her naked the moment they'd tumbled through the door—it felt like a lifetime ago—and knelt at her feet to bury his face in all that glorious heat.

It was certainly the first image which had raced into his own head the moment they'd stepped into his apartment.

It didn't help that she'd been dressed to kill that night, too. In a dress which had been infinitely sexy, if not quite as stunning as the creation she was wearing now. An emerald green thing, which complemented her dark skin tones to perfection.

Before he could stop himself, his mind leapt to the question of whether she was wearing the same delicate bra and thong set. And were those infinitely long legs encased in the same style of sexy lace-top hold-ups?

God, what was the matter with him?

Malachi fought to drag his mind back to the present and failed, almost despairing of himself—until he saw the quickening, jerky pulse thud at the base of her elegant neck and realised that his wasn't the only mind that had wandered.

Good! Satisfaction pounded through him. *Maybe he could use that to his advantage.*

'We should have this conversation somewhere a little more comfortable than standing in the entrance hall, don't you think, Saskia?' he murmured, moving to usher her through to the main lounge.

'I seriously doubt this is going to be a comfortable discussion wherever we have it,' she shot back crisply.

He had to force himself to keep sauntering into the living area without glancing around, as though he felt as casual and self-contained as he miraculously appeared.

'Surely all the more reason not to exacerbate things, then?'

Moving around the space, he busied himself

with a drink he didn't even want for himself, and a bottle of the mineral water he recalled she favoured, then threw himself into a soft leather chair and deliberately stretched out, as if he was at ease. Her eyes widened, even as she drew her lips into a thin line and lifted her nose ever so slightly in the air.

Malachi didn't realise he'd been holding his breath until she finally, stiffly, followed him into the room.

She eyed the leather sofa—where even now he could remember laying her out almost reverently, before finally burying his face in her sweet, intense heat—and she perched, rather awkwardly, on its arm. The mineral water was left untouched on the table between them.

'What now?' she repeated sharply, but he didn't miss the glimmer of nervousness.

The problem was that he didn't really know the answer. She was pregnant with his baby and she'd been so afraid that he wouldn't want to know that firstly she hadn't even told him, and secondly she'd tried to absolve him of all responsibility.

Fresh anger surged through him, and suddenly Malachi found himself talking without even realising what he was saying.

'*Now*, Saskia,' he bit out, 'you will move in with me and I will provide for you and for our baby.'

'I'm sorry…what did you just say?'

She looked utterly stupefied. Exactly the way *he* ought to feel. He could hardly believe the words that had come out of his mouth—*move in with him*—where had that even come from? It was ludicrous. Sheer folly.

And yet there wasn't an atom of him that wanted to take it back.

He ought to feel numb.

Detached.

Instead he suspected that what he was feeling—for the first time in a long, long time—was alive.

And that made no sense either.

Even now, after everything she'd said, it was taking more self-control than he felt it ought to not to reach out and haul her to him. He wanted her with a ferociousness he didn't recognise in himself.

A yearning.

And he didn't yearn. He wasn't desperate. Not ever.

At least not any more. He'd left that nonsense behind along with his childhood. Yearning for a better life, a kinder childhood, a fairer world— all of which he'd quickly learned wouldn't simply come to him. If he wanted them, he'd have to take them. Claim them. Seize them. In business and in his personal life. Fighting with every fibre of his body—even as an eight-year-old—to keep himself and Sol off the Social Services radar.

He hadn't stopped fighting since.

Conquering. Annexing. Discarding.

And people thanked him for it.

Companies were all the better for it even when he stripped them down and walked away from them.

Yes, it suited him just fine.

But *his baby*? That was one thing on which he could never turn his back. He knew that now with a certainty that rocked him to his core. In an instant all the fears which had crowded his head—his heart—had simply...*vanished*.

He didn't feel resentment, or fear, or bitterness when he thought of the two of them in his life. He felt...*odd*.

But not a *bad* odd.

Malachi shoved the unfamiliar sensations aside roughly. They only brought with them a sense of confusion, and that was the last thing he wanted.

'I don't think you're thinking straight, Malachi,' she managed defiantly.

'On the contrary. I'm thinking perfectly straight.'

'You can't really expect me to move in with you as though...as though...we're going to be some kind of...happy family,' she stuttered, flailing her arms around a little too much for someone who was trying to sound in control.

'I don't see why not,' he drawled, as though there *wasn't* a pounding so loud in his chest that it might as well have been a roll of thunder right overhead. 'We've made a baby together, Saskia. In my book that makes us some kind of family— so why not make it a happy one?'

'That's…ludicrous.'

'More ludicrous than you thinking you could cut me out of my own baby's life?'

She stopped, swallowed hard, but then looked him in the eye. 'I apologise for that but, like I said, I intended to tell you until I realised you were avoiding me and I lost my nerve. But this… moving in together…it won't work.'

'I disagree.'

'I want my child to have stability in its life— people who will always be there, come what may. Not someone who decides after a few months or years that it isn't for them after all.'

'I beg your pardon?'

He could see her skin prickle at the unmistakably dangerous edge to his tone, but she continued anyway.

'I want my baby to feel loved, and happy, and secure. Always. I know I can provide all of that for my child. I will never walk away or abandon it.'

'And you believe I will?' Barely restrained fury arced between them, virtually scorching her with its intensity. 'I can assure you that will never happen.'

'You say that now…'

There was no rancour in her voice, and he could tell she was trying to project a quiet inner strength, but he could hear the faint quiver and see the slight tremor of her hands.

'But however good your intentions are at this moment in time, Malachi, you never wanted any of this—you're happy being a bachelor. What happens when you decide that being a father isn't for you after all?'

'That won't happen,' he gritted out.

But she continued as though he hadn't even spoken. 'You'll leave. Maybe it will happen slowly, maybe overnight, but either way my child will feel abandoned.'

'*Our* child,' he growled. 'And I will not do that to our baby. I do not simply walk away from my commitments or my responsibilities.'

'I'm sure you don't. You don't build a business empire like MIG International unless you're dedicated, single-minded. But this is a baby—not a business. It's a very different prospect.'

'Be very careful, Saskia, about what you think I do and don't understand.' His tone was well moderated, but he could feel the restrained emotion in every syllable.

'Then tell me!' she exploded unexpectedly. 'Tell me something about Malachi Gunn that I don't know. Because you never told me a single thing that weekend.'

His jaw was locked so tight it was almost painful, but he couldn't seem to loosen it however hard he tried. A storm was building inside him, silent but nonetheless lethal. And still Saskia pressed on.

'Tell me something that isn't some morsel of PR carefully crafted for the world at large.' Her voice rose despite her obvious attempts to be calm. 'I challenge you.'

It was all so close to the bone that Malachi was sure she was scraping him, fracturing him, splintering him. Worse, he was almost tempted to answer her. To tell her something about his godawful childhood that no one but he and Sol knew. To make her understand this sudden, driving need to ensure that his child had the kind of family life he had never enjoyed.

Only he wasn't quite sure he entirely understood it himself.

He struggled to maintain his composure. 'The way you told me something personal about yourself?' he countered. 'We both have our reasons for keeping people at arm's length. I recommend you don't ask me questions you yourself wouldn't be prepared to answer.'

'That's precisely my point, though...' She lifted her hand, then dropped it. Confusion flooded through her gaze, as though she knew the tension was escalating but had no idea how to stop it. 'We both like our privacy. How do you see us raising a child together? There's nothing real between us.'

He opened his mouth to reply and then his eyes caught sight of her hands, moving subconsciously to cradle her belly, her baby. *Their* baby. And they were sitting here arguing.

How had things degenerated like this?

Abruptly Malachi reached forward and poured out her water. The sound of it pouring from the bottle into her glass filled the room, and he concentrated on the noise the ice cubes made as they clinked and tinkled together. Anything to distract himself for even a moment.

Then he reached out to hand her the glass and their fingers brushed. It was like a shot of pure adrenaline. He might as well have been dancing out of his own skin. And judging by the expression clouding Saskia's face he wasn't the only one.

So much for *nothing real* between them.

He moved back to his seat, took a moment to compose himself. When he spoke again his voice was low, firm. 'I didn't bring you here to row with you, Saskia. I brought you because I wanted somewhere private for us to discuss what happens next.'

'Discuss?' she asked.

But he noted that her tone was softer now.

His attempt to defuse the situation had clearly worked. At least to some degree.

'Or for you to command and for me to listen?' she went on.

'That will very much depend on whether you accept what I say, *zvyozdochka*, or decide to argue against it.'

Zvyozdochka. The endearment he had used that weekend slipped out before he could stop himself, causing Saskia to snap her head up.

He cursed himself for giving too much away.

'I didn't think you accepted people arguing with you?' she challenged softly.

'I don't,' he bit out. 'So allow me to tell you exactly what is going to happen, Saskia.'

He watched her swallow. Hard. Then she folded her arms over her chest. Nonetheless, he didn't miss the tremor that rippled through her body. Just as he noticed that she didn't say anything to stop him.

'You are carrying my child. *Mine*. Whatever you might think that idiot ex-fiancé of yours would have done, or wanted to do, is of no consequence to me. I don't care about him, or the life you thought you were building with him. I don't care about your broken heart or lack of trust. I care that my baby won't suffer because of your hang-ups.'

Or his own, if he were honest.

Though Malachi chose not to voice that.

'Good to know,' she choked out. 'Anything else?'

'Yes, as it happens...' He had no idea what he was saying, just knew that words were flowing from him as though they'd been there all along. 'Forget just moving in with me. You will be my wife.'

It hung there between them in the shocked silence. For how long, he had no idea.

And then Saskia gave an indelicate snort. 'That's even more preposterous than your first suggestion.'

An hour ago he might have agreed. Half an hour ago. But now he'd begun to get used to the idea.

Far more quickly than he might have expected to.

'I disagree.'

'We're not living in the last century. I don't have to be married to have a child,' she declared vehemently. And then, almost as an afterthought, added less emphatically, 'Besides, I don't want to be your wife.'

As if she had belatedly realized that was something she *ought* to have thought, rather than something she actually *had* thought.

'Marriage is not an institution that I thought I would ever enter,' was all he could answer. 'But for the sake of your baby, this *will* happen. Our child will know only a close family unit.'

She sucked in a shocked breath. 'You can't be serious.'

'Do I look like I am joking?'

She opened her mouth, closed it again, then shot back at him. 'And in this ridiculous scenario of yours, do you imagine we will be sleeping together, like we're really a couple?'

He could tell she regretted the words as soon as they came out of her mouth, and he knew precisely why.

'How interesting that that's where your mind went, Saskia,' he purred. 'Though I assume *sleeping together* is a euphemism for having sex, since I'll remind you that we didn't actually do much of the former.'

She shifted in her seat and then glowered at him.

She didn't answer. She didn't need to. She was moving restlessly again, clearly jumpy, and he knew in that moment that she was remembering how incredible it had been between them—because he was remembering it, too.

It hummed and whispered through the air around them. The way her body had fitted to his as if she'd been crafted just for him. The way she'd responded to his touch. The way he'd burned with a fire which had never seemed to die down.

'You're mad if you think that's going to happen again...' The words finally tumbled out,

sharp and jerky, as if even she didn't quite believe what she was saying.

'You protest too much, Saskia. Especially
when your body betrays you. Or did you think
I hadn't noticed the way it reacts to me? *Still.*'

He relished the expression which poured out
of those rich nut-brown eyes, that tongue flicking over her lips, reminding him of the way it
had slid over almost every inch of him a few
months ago.

Even the memory made him tighten as surely
as if she'd been raking his body with her fingers,
and he grabbed hold of it. Because if he held
on to their physical attraction, their undeniable
chemistry, then he wouldn't have to consider that
there might be more to the way he felt about her
than merely the superficial.

He was so caught up in his thoughts that it
took a moment for him to realise she was still
addressing him.

'I won't sleep with you again, Malachi.' She
punched her chin out for emphasis. 'You can't
make me just because you're insisting we marry
as though we're back in the fifties.'

'I have no intention of *making* you do anything,' he commented dryly. 'You will *want*
to, Saskia. More than that, you will beg me to
take you.'

'Because you know my body better than I do,

I suppose?' She lifted one nonchalant shoulder and shook her hair out.

He felt it like a caress against the hardest part of himself.

'I think we both know that your body *longs* right now,' he growled. 'Why you should go on denying it is a mystery.'

'Because you're such a prize, of course,' Saskia bit back, a little of her former feistiness returning.

His grin widened that little bit more, and she shivered as though she could actually *feel* those bared teeth against her skin. He found he rather liked the notion.

'So I've been told.'

'I imagine there are several million things informing that opinion,' she managed pointedly.

'No doubt,' he agreed readily enough. 'It's the way of the world, is it not? Although I think we both know that it isn't simply my multimillion-pound fortune alone which attracts women. It wasn't what attracted you, after all. So, what *did* attract you, Saskia?'

She shivered—a deep ripple of anticipation which he could read like other people could read a book. Despite her attempts to remain at arm's length, she couldn't deny their mutual attraction any more than he could.

'You were just my rebound,' she managed

weakly. 'I told you that the first night and you agreed.'

'Indeed.' He dipped his head. 'Except now you're carrying my baby, and I don't intend to be kept out of its life.'

Her gaze simmered. And yet somehow he knew that he was sliding under Saskia's skin all the deeper, and that she was tempted. Just as he was. He felt her everywhere, and it didn't help that he could see she was teetering over the precipice of agreeing.

'So you've said. But…'

'But…?' he encouraged, when she didn't continue.

'But that doesn't mean marriage is the solution. As though I'm just a problem for you to solve like one of your business deals. And marriage certainly shouldn't be a business deal with benefits, as you're suggesting.'

'All right—so what, in your opinion, *should* marriage be, *zvyozdochka*?'

'Forget it.' She shook her head.

'I don't think I will,' he told her lazily. 'I find I'm almost on tenterhooks to hear your answer.'

'You're impossible.'

'Quite probably. So, tell me what marriage should be.'

It was insane. No one else could spar with him the way she could. Or, more to the point, no one else made him feel the way she did when she sparred with him, even when she wasn't even trying. She made him feel almost...*predatory*.

'You realise that the more you evade the question the more fascinated I become?'

'Then you're only setting yourself up for disappointment. I have no great revelation for you. Just my rather ordinary opinion.'

'I would hardly call you *rather ordinary*,' he countered, his gaze sweeping over her as though she'd laid down a fresh challenge.

'For pity's sake...' She exhaled, but then she ducked her eyes from his and he knew he had her.

He pressed his advantage home. 'What is marriage to you, Saskia?'

'Marriage is... Well, it's love. *True* love.'

'Like you had with that cheating ex-fiancé of yours?'

It occurred to him, a fraction too late, that some part of him was jealous.

Ridiculous. He didn't do jealous. And yet...

'No, not like Andy,' Saskia refuted hotly. 'He was an idiot for treating me the way he did, and I was even more of one for letting him.'

It shouldn't, yet her admission buoyed Malachi.

'Then what?'

'I... I don't know.'

'Something Hollywood, perhaps? Glittery and

perfect? I hate to burst your bubble, Saskia, but that's just for the movies—it doesn't really exist.'

'I'm well aware of that,' she managed hotly. 'My mother was big screen royalty, so I've lived it, remember?'

'Then what?' he pushed again. 'Perhaps something more akin to the passionate, heady thing your parents had? That well-documented great romance?'

He was deliberately needling her, but still Malachi wasn't prepared for the bleak look which suddenly pierced her gaze. A split second of pain which he could read only too acutely, could recognise only too easily. It sliced through him, too, spiked and merciless, before Saskia yanked her features into a semblance of equilibrium.

Malachi faltered. It was widely known that Saskia's parents had been madly in love—the Hollywood dream. Even their deaths had been considered the embodiment of romance: dying in each other's arms at the side of a road.

But it wouldn't have been romantic for the young Saskia. What the hell had he been thinking, raking up memories which must be hurtful? And there was something about the expression in her eyes which warned him that the pain he'd seen ran even deeper than losing her parents.

He'd experienced enough to know that there was something else. Something more. Something the rest of the world didn't seem to know.

He sought something to say, but nothing seemed right.

'Passion is overrated,' she managed, breaking the silence for herself. 'We had passion, but it doesn't mean anything. It was a one-night stand. It's over. I don't want you like that any more.'

Something kicked hard in his chest. 'I think we both know that's a lie.'

And then he was right there in front of her, unable to stop himself from reaching out and sliding one hand into those thick, glossy black curls that he imagined he could feel sweeping over his chest as they'd done every time she'd raked that wicked mouth of hers over his chest—and lower.

He tilted his head to look up into her eyes. Their rich, expressive depths were spilling over with unspoken longing, confirming all his suspicions. And still he had to force the next words out.

Testing her? Or himself?

He couldn't quite tell.

'One word, Saskia,' he rasped. 'One word from you and I'll let you go and never speak of it again. So I'd advise you to be sure that's what you really want.'

'I...'

The sound was low, halting. It vibrated around his chest and echoed off the walls, affording him some sense of victory. Clearly she could no longer pretend that she didn't ache for him, just as he wanted her with such intensity that he almost couldn't think straight.

His mind raced ahead before he could rein it in. Perhaps if they indulged this one last time it might sate the hunger which had been eating away inside him ever since this incomparable woman had left his bed three months ago.

Perhaps.

'I didn't quite catch that, Saskia. Was that another failed attempt at denial?'

He lifted his hand and brushed her cheek—the faintest of contacts and yet it ripped through him.

Saskia sucked in a sharp breath as if to echo it. 'Malachi…'

'Repeat it, if you will,' he enjoined, all too aware that his leaden voice betrayed him but not even caring any more.

And then her eyes flashed. They locked with his in unmistakable defiance, just as they had for a moment back on that promenade. A kick of that spirited, feisty Saskia he recognised only too well. It was like a shot of pure lust straight through to his sex.

'Fine,' she gritted out. 'I still want you. I know I shouldn't, but I do. Is that what you wanted to hear?'

'It's a start.' He lowered his head slowly towards her, pulled by some invisible thread which seemed to be as delicate and as strong as spider's silk.

'We can't…' She shook her head weakly. 'This isn't about another roll in the hay. There's a baby now—*our* baby. The fact of whether we still have chemistry or not is irrelevant.'

'I beg to differ,' Malachi growled.

And he was unable to stop himself from closing the gap and finally covering her mouth with his, revelling in the way Saskia surrendered to him in an instant. Her lithe body moulded to his, and her arms snaked around his neck as if they knew her mind better than her brain did.

And Malachi indulged. Deepening the kiss and giving in to the savage, raw ache that roared inside him. The inconceivable *need* he felt to be with her—inside her—over and over again.

She was his.

It thundered through his veins even as he struggled to comprehend what it meant. She was carrying his baby. Never again would another man touch her the way that he did. Be with her the way he was.

She was *his*.

Even if he didn't fully grasp what that meant.

Even if a part of him knew—*knew*—that he was about to complicate things in a way that he had been avoiding his entire adult life.

CHAPTER FIVE

IT WAS ELECTRIC. *He* was electric. Just as it had been three months ago.

Better.

Saskia melted into him in an instant, all her tentative resolve gone, and the painful memory of her parents' death was dissipated the moment Malachi's lips touched hers.

She wanted him with an intensity that should have terrified her. On some level, it did. And yet she couldn't stop—couldn't drag her mouth from the thrilling slide of his; couldn't unwind her arms from around his neck, where they'd slid almost of their own volition.

She didn't *want* to stop.

He gathered her to him, lifting her up and pulling her legs around his waist, running one big, callused hand along the length of her exposed thigh as the long side slit of her dress fell away. And when she locked her heels together, drawing herself that bit tighter to him, he made a low rumble of approval deep in his throat, and it rolled through her like the most delicious storm.

Supporting her with one hand, the other hand brushing the hair gently from her cheek as his mouth still plundered hers, Malachi carried her through his loft-style apartment. Everything in her jolted in anticipation of the intimate reunion she'd imagined over and over in her head, but had never believed would actually happen.

'Last chance, Saskia,' he muttered, his voice hard and dark as he shouldered his way into the plush master suite and carried her to the bed.

She wondered what it had cost him to drag his mouth from hers and stand there now, so still and unmoving.

Could she have stopped like that?

She doubted it. Every inch of her was on fire. She *ached* between her legs. Even her lips tingled, as though objecting to the loss of his mouth on hers.

'I don't want you to stop,' she managed, and the sense of relief was almost overwhelming as he offered barely a grunt of confirmation before lowering her onto the bed.

And then he was pushing the long skirt of her gown up to her hips, deliberately slowly, his hands grazing her thighs, higher and higher. His lips followed—languid, indulgent kisses, all stopping just short of where she yearned for his touch the most.

Again and again he repeated the motion. Up one side, then down the other, so close she could feel his breath brush over her molten heat through her lacy underwear, but never touching her. When she thought she could take it no longer she arched up slightly, only for Malachi to slide his hands under her backside and hold her in place.

'Malachi…'

'Patience, *zvyozdochka*…'

She could hear the amused smile even without seeing it.

'All in good time.'

'This *is* in so-called *good* time,' she grumbled.

'On the contrary. I find I want more time to get reacquainted with every millimetre of you.' Backing off the bed, he ran his tongue down from her thigh to her knee, making her tremble all over. 'Especially these long, incredibly sexy legs of yours, which you wrapped so tightly right around me when I drove deep inside you.'

She remembered. Lord, how she remembered.

But before she could answer Malachi was moving back up again, his lips, his tongue, his teeth, trailing a fiery blaze to the apex of her legs. Only this time he didn't stop short. And he didn't skirt over her core.

This time he bent his head and licked his way straight into her molten heat.

Saskia cried out instantly, helpless to stop

her body from writhing under his expert touch. He was chasing her to the edge far faster than she could have imagined—but then she'd been dreaming of being back here in Malachi's bed ever since she'd left it, three months ago.

She was dimly aware that in her dreams it hadn't been just about her. In her dreams Malachi had been just as close to spiralling as she felt now. But then he lifted her backside with his hands, his tongue working a kind of magic inside her, and every thought went out of her head. There was only the pure sensation of what he was doing to her *right now*.

She had no idea how long they remained there. How long he played with her, toyed with her. Only knew that her body was revelling in every minute of it. There would never be anyone else for her like Malachi—she'd known that truth even before she'd realised she was pregnant— so if this was to be their one and only revisiting of history, she intended to enjoy every last second of it.

All too soon a delicious tremor began to work its way through Saskia's body, rippling out from her core to the tips of her toes, her fingers, her head. And Malachi responded accordingly, increasing his wicked rhythm and changing angles until she was grasping at the bedding for purchase, the wildest little sounds escaping from her.

And then he closed his lips over the very centre of her need and sucked. *Hard.*

Saskia exploded.

A detonation of sensations coursed through her entire body and she shamelessly rode them out. Soaring on every last one of them. It might as well have been a lifetime before she came back down to earth, exhausted, boneless, and not even able to draw a steady breath.

By the time she finally came to and sat up, gingerly, Malachi was watching her. She recognised his dark, intense expression—*desire*—and it sent a thrill of pleasure down her spine.

'Now, I rather think I should return the compliment…' she managed hoarsely, reaching for his hands, which he duly extended, and allowing him to draw her to her feet, before turning her back to him and pulling her hair over her shoulder to expose the pearl buttons at the back of her gown. 'If you wouldn't mind?'

'If you insist.'

His gravelly voice was distinctively loaded and intent, and she knew she wasn't imagining the faint shake in his hands as he began to release one tiny button after another.

It gave her a sense of elation…almost of *power*…that a man with the kind of formidable, controlled reputation in business that Malachi had should be so close to the edge with her.

It felt like an age before the buttons were all

undone, but as Saskia felt the halterneck fall, she turned slowly, allowing the dress to puddle at her feet before stepping elegantly out, and Malachi's eyes went almost black as he reached for her, his hands cupping the faintest swell of her abdomen.

'Actually, I rather think…' she licked her lips, her eyes locking with his as she sank to her knees '…that it's my turn.'

It took him a moment to register what she was doing. Long enough for her to unsnap his belt and for him to hear the sinful sound of her undoing his zip before he moved his hands to cover hers and still them.

'No…' He barely recognised his hoarse voice. 'You can't.'

'Why not?' she murmured, and the heat from her breath rushed over his sex, making him tighten and ache desperately.

He could scarcely form the words. 'You're pregnant, *zvyozdochka*.'

'Ah…' she murmured, twisting her hands from under his and releasing him from the confines of his boxers before he could even react. 'And somehow that makes me fragile and innocent in your book?'

'Saskia…' he warned, trailing off as she coiled her fingers around his sex and stroked all that velvet and steel.

'Let me assure you, Malachi, that there is

nothing fragile about being pregnant. If anything, it makes me bolder than ever.'

Then, before he could answer, she tipped her head forward and took him straight into her mouth. Hot, and deep, and positively indecent.

When he looked down she was looking right back at him, his sex in her mouth and the naughtiest of smirks curving her lips.

He meant to stop her. To pull her to her feet. Instead he found himself lacing his fingers through her curls and holding on as though he might topple if he didn't.

He thought he was going to explode right there.

Again and again she tasted him, licked him, sucked him. Her tongue, her teeth and her wicked little fingers were all working in perfect lazy synchronicity to stoke that fire in him, hotter and higher.

It was incredible. *She* was incredible.

Malachi had never felt so wholly at someone's mercy and he found, with Saskia, he rather liked it.

And then suddenly it wasn't lazy any more. He was catapulting towards the edge. Closer and closer. Her mouth was so damned wet and hot.

'No,' he ground out, pulling himself out of her mouth although it was delicious agony to do so. 'Not like this.'

Scooping her up, he carried her to the bed and

threw her down, shedding his clothes as fast as he could.

Finally—*at last*—he was covering her body with his, skin to skin, as he dropped his head to her jawline and trailed kisses all the way along it and down that glorious neckline, with deliberate care and attention. And then he turned his attention to her collarbone, and the sensitive hollow at the base of her neck. First one side and then the other.

Malachi could feel her nipples, hard and proud, chafing against his chest. He revelled in the way her breath hitched in her throat with every slide of his tongue. And still he took his time.

By the time he'd worked his way down her chest, to draw one exquisite nipple into his mouth, Saskia was gasping and locking her arms around him, trying to pull him down onto her properly.

It took all he had to resist her.

This was her moment, and he wanted it to be perfect.

He drew whorls around her nipples with his tongue. First one, then the other. Then he propped himself over her and let his hands take over.

He was so damned hard it was almost painful, but still he didn't let her touch him, however much she arched and writhed beneath him.

And then he was reaching down between

them. Letting his fingers dance over her belly, over the softest of curves where his baby lay within her, over her hip and down her thigh.

His. All his.

'Malachi...' she groaned. 'Touch me...'

'Patience, *zvyozdochka*,' he rasped. 'All in good time.'

The truth was, if he touched her too early he feared he wouldn't hold out.

It had never, *never* been like this before. Only that first time with Saskia, and he'd been fantasising about this moment ever since.

He built up the rhythm in her. Higher and faster. Until eventually he reached down between her legs and let his fingers sink into all that sweet, molten heat.

She sighed and shuddered instantly. 'More,' she moaned. 'I need more.'

And, God help him, he needed to hear it.

'Tell me exactly what you need, *zvyozdochka*,' he commanded. 'I want to hear you say it.'

She groaned again, a low, needy sound which ripped right through him. He couldn't help it. Nestling between her legs, he flexed himself against her wet core.

'You, Malachi,' she muttered, opening her legs and arching as his tip slipped inside. 'Inside me.'

He couldn't stand it any longer. He thrust inside her. Slick, hard, deep. Just as Saskia wrapped her legs around him and clung on.

In and out, and she lifted up and met him stroke for stroke. The only sound was their ragged breathing, and every so often a deep, sensual groan. And then she lifted her legs higher, locking them tightly around his waist and twisting, so he plunged in that little bit further, and Malachi knew he was lost.

Just as he reached down between them, playing with the centre of her need, he heard her cry out his name. Her entire body shuddered, then tensed, then stilled, and he flicked his fingers expertly.

Saskia screamed, calling his name and toppling over the edge. And still he kept going, flinging her straight back over every time she thought she was done, until the final time, when she slid her hands down his back and cupped his buttocks, pulling him into her with such force he couldn't tell where he ended and she began.

This time when she shattered around him his name was on her lips. He drove himself home and followed her into oblivion.

CHAPTER SIX

MALACHI CURSED UNDER his breath. A filthy Russian curse he remembered his mother using—if not in the beginning, then certainly a lot towards the end.

Saskia was carrying his child.

His baby.

And he'd forgotten. All he'd been thinking about was getting inside her again, just like three months ago.

But this wasn't then—this was *now*. She was the mother of his unborn child and everything had changed. He was going to look after them. That was his responsibility. But responsibility and personal life were different things, and that meant there had to be boundaries. He couldn't go blurring the lines by being intimate with Saskia. There had to be rules.

He ignored the voice in the back of his brain asking *Why?* Needling him. Whispering that if there weren't rules, he wouldn't have to keep his hands off the woman who was even now still naked in his master suite.

And, God, how a part of him ached to spin around, go back in there and take her. Over and over again.

'Weakness!' he muttered, slamming his fist on the countertop as he marched into the kitchen to get himself a long, cold glass of water, when what he really needed was a very long, very icy-cold shower.

Though privately he doubted even that would do the trick. Saskia had got under his skin the first time they'd met and he'd been trying to eject her ever since.

In some ways the appalling misstep he'd made tonight had been inevitable. And if he didn't have those rules in place it could just as easily happen again. He couldn't allow it.

He *wouldn't* allow it.

Being out of control was something he would never accept. And there was nothing controlled about this dark, needy thing which swirled inside him whenever he was with Saskia. Hell, whenever he even thought about her.

It felt altogether too much like powerlessness. And he'd sworn, back when he was eight years old, that when he grew up he would never allow anything to make him feel powerless again. Which meant showing no emotion.

Emotions were a bad thing. They were what

made things start to unravel. His parents had loved each other—and hated each other, for that matter—with such intense passion that their relationship had been an emotional roller-coaster. And not just for them, but for him and his brother, too.

Malachi didn't know how much his brother, Sol, remembered about those very early years, if he remembered anything, but for him it had been draining. He'd never known whether their parents were going to be there at any given time, to remember to cook a meal, or give them a bath, or even just tuck them in to bed at a decent hour.

But that had been nothing compared to the powerlessness he'd felt when their father had died. Their mother had been unable to cope with the loss, and spiralling into drug addiction had been the only means of escape she could see.

It had fallen to Malachi to keep things together. From looking after the house to taking care of his baby brother. By the time he'd turned eight he'd been doing whatever it took to survive, to put food on the table for him and his brother, and to keep the local dealers away from his junkie mother.

Something ugly twisted and flipped deep inside him—something which a lesser man might have taken to be regret, maybe sadness, possibly even grief—but Malachi slammed it down in an instant.

God, why was he even thinking of this now?

It belonged in the past.

This was Sol's fault, for raking it all up the other day at the hospital. Stirring up old memories both of them were better off forgetting.

There was no point in *what ifs*. He'd learned that as a kid, the moment he'd taken up the reins as the adult of the house. He'd had rules, and he'd taken control of everything. His single-mindedness had enabled him to drag himself and Sol out of the gutter. He'd built MIG International after learning investment strategies from the internet, and he'd sent Sol to medical school.

Saskia threatened all of that. Or, more to the point, his lack of focus when it came to this one woman threatened all of that.

He forgot himself around her.

And that couldn't happen.

Things had changed; she was carrying his baby and he couldn't let his desire for her make him forget his responsibility as a father. He absolutely would *not* put this child through anything like what his parents had put him and Sol through.

He would not give in to that primal part of him which seemed to crave her so very greatly.

He was better than that. And any child of his deserved more than that.

'Malachi...? Why did you leave like that?'

He didn't realise she'd followed him out, hadn't heard her footsteps coming down the hall until he heard her quiet, shaky voice. Despite all his internal cautioning his chest tightened at the mere sound of her near him. And if he hadn't known better he might have actually believed his heart gave a kick of delight.

What the hell was he playing at?

Malachi jabbed his finger on the countertop. 'That should never have happened.'

He could spout about honour and legitimacy and protection all he liked, but he suspected that the real truth of it was far less altruistic. He was being led by something far baser, far more primal. He was being led by his unextinguished desire for Saskia. She was like the worst kind of drug. One taste of her and he'd been hungering for her ever since, craving her in a way which was entirely too much out of his control for Malachi's liking.

And he was *never* out of control.

Yet here he was, desperate to keep her here before she remembered her own mind and walked away from him, just like she had at the end of that weekend.

'I won't marry you,' she said belligerently.

Malachi bared his teeth in what he hoped would pass for a grim smile. 'Yes, Saskia, you will.'

Because his child would *never* have anyone look at him as though he was *less* than anyone else.

'You think that just because you have money you can order people to do whatever you see fit?'

He hadn't anticipated this show of temper.

'It won't work on me. You're not the only one to have come from money. To be used to getting your own way. I can be just as obstinate, too.'

He wanted to tell her that he hadn't come from money. That he had scraped and struggled for every penny he had ever made. But he didn't. Because he knew it mattered to his brother—more than it ever had to himself—not to reveal the true depths of their childhood.

It took him a moment to realise he had hit a nerve.

Interesting.

'We've been through this, Saskia, have we not? I understand that you're the daughter of Hollywood royalty and that your childhood must have been a fairy tale. You had two parents who loved each other right up until the last. But this isn't a perfect movie story. This is real life.'

And he told himself that he didn't covet any of it—because if he hadn't experienced the hell of his own childhood he wouldn't be where he was today.

'Of course,' she managed tightly, her face shutting down just as it had a matter of hours ago.

And Malachi resolved in that instant to uncover just what it was that Saskia was hiding.

He knew he should put a stop to it immediately, but found he couldn't. What was it he'd just been saying about rules and control? Yet in reality he was so far out of his comfort zone he scarcely recognised himself.

Worse. A part of him didn't even seem to care.

He shoved his hands in his pockets, balling them into fists, as though that might somehow help him hold on to his own sanity. He had to do something to recover his equilibrium.

'I think it would be best if I take you home whilst I decide how best to handle this situation.'

'I am not a *situation* that needs to be handled,' she hissed incredulously.

'I would beg to differ.'

People didn't challenge you when you were the boss of a multinational organisation. They certainly didn't talk back or banter. But Saskia bit back with whatever was on her mind—rather like Sol did—and Malachi had to admit it was refreshing.

'And now, as much as this conversation is diverting, I think it's best if I take you home.'

Even though every fibre in his body was screaming for him not to let her leave.

Or maybe *because* every fibre in him was screaming for him not to let her leave.

'And then what?' she demanded.

He didn't have the answer to that. He only knew that whilst she was here he couldn't think straight. He needed time—and a little space— to come up with a workable solution. One that didn't put him straight in temptation's path.

'I'll let you know.' He shrugged, moving towards the door. 'When I'm ready.'

'Hi, I'm Saskia, the doctor who has taken over Caleb's case.' Saskia smiled gently at the frightened-looking woman with her five-month-old baby. 'This must be Caleb, and you're Mum?'

The woman nodded jerkily.

Saskia could only empathise. The woman had brought her baby in the previous night and he had been diagnosed with bronchiolitis, moderate in severity. But, according to the handover team, less than hour ago he'd begun to show signs of deterioration.

'So, the previous doctor told you that my colleague, Maria, is going to start this little man on high oxygen flow?'

'Yes. Will that cure him?' the woman choked out.

'It should help Caleb to breathe a little easier,'

explained Saskia. 'Are you here on your own? Is there anyone who can be with you?'

The woman shook her head.

'No one. It's just the two of us. Caleb wasn't planned, and when I found out I was pregnant, Tom—Caleb's dad—didn't want to know. We'd been together for a year. I didn't expect him to propose or anything. But I didn't think he'd leave us without a word.'

'I'm so sorry,' Saskia offered, not sure what else to say. 'Well, we're here for you and your son. Try not to worry—the oxygen should help. I'll check on him in about an hour or so to make sure that it is, okay?'

'Okay.'

Saskia pulled the curtain out of the way and stepped out, confirming her intentions with Maria before moving on to check the next priority on her ward round.

But her head was spinning.

She'd spent the past week since she'd left Malachi's apartment throwing herself into work. Doing everything she could to keep her mind off the man who was the father of her unborn baby.

She'd convinced herself that she'd made the right decision in rejecting his marriage proposal, but now, after that revelation from her young patient's mother, she was seriously doubting herself.

Whatever else she could say about her and

Malachi, she couldn't say that he didn't want to know about their baby. They weren't even a couple, yet he'd instantly expected to be part of their life. Had practically insisted on it.

Had she been thinking of *her* best interests or her unborn baby's when she'd dismissed Malachi's marriage proposal so scornfully? It wasn't as though they couldn't stand each other. In fact, quite the opposite.

Without warning, images of Malachi touching her—his hands, his mouth—flashed into her head, leaving her body searing. Feeling as though it might combust at any moment. The way it had been doing every time she'd thought of him over the past few months.

Only this time it was much, much worse. Because with each week that had gone by she'd managed to persuade herself that she was exaggerating quite how good he'd been. Quite how skilled.

But that repeat performance last week had offered her a whole host of new experiences and, even more galling, had only proved to her that her imagination *hadn't* been overselling Malachi's talent in playing her body. If anything, her memories had seriously underplayed his artistry and the devastating effect he had on her.

And, for all her posturing, the simple truth was that she longed for more. She *craved* it. And that couldn't be a good thing to want with the man who was supposed to have been her rebound one-night stand.

What if marriage to Malachi wasn't so bad after all?

You're just having a wobble, she told herself firmly, heading for the nurses' station, which was mercifully deserted, and gripping hold of the melamine surface so hard that her knuckles went white.

She was having a scan this afternoon. No doubt that was why seeing Caleb's mother had frightened her when she thought about having the baby alone.

As much as she might like to pretend otherwise, she was already watching the door for Malachi, and it didn't matter that it was at least four hours too early. He'd told her it was *'all or nothing'*, but she didn't know whether to believe him. A part of her hoped he would be there. But now she'd seen Caleb and his mother and she'd realised that it was foolish of her to assume Malachi would come after she'd told him he didn't have to.

And yet it had frightened her to think that he might not.

What she ought to focus on was the fact that she wasn't Caleb's mother, and Malachi wasn't this Tom. There was no reason for her to panic and rush into a marriage neither of them would have even considered if she hadn't been pregnant, as though this was last century.

She ignored the tiny voice needling her, telling her that any woman who didn't consider marriage to a man as successful and stunning and all-round masculine as Malachi Gunn had to be a little bit mad.

'Saskia?'

The shrill sound of Babette had Saskia squeezing her eyes shut. Was there no shift she could work in this hospital without that woman seeming to dog her?

'Are you all right? You aren't going to faint again, are you?'

Plastering a bright smile on her face, Saskia squared her shoulders and spun around.

'No, Babette, I'm quite all right.'

The woman didn't even have the decency to disguise her disappointment.

'Your concern is really quite touching, though.'

And she strode off to her next patient before Babette could answer.

Mercifully, the rest of the morning passed quickly. Between rounds and routine jobs she also saw several chest infections, some minor injuries, an undescended testicle and a hip misalignment. Just the kind of busy morning to keep her brain perfectly occupied.

So by the time she'd made sure everything was

handed over for the next half hour or so, there were a mere ten minutes until her scan.

And no sign of Malachi.

Her heart beat out a frenetic rhythm in her chest and her stomach dipped, but she told herself that she was fine, and rubbed her hand gently over her abdomen. It was startling how, despite her pregnancy not starting to show yet, she felt attached to her baby. He or she wasn't even planned, and yet she already couldn't imagine not being pregnant.

And in less than an hour she would be meeting her baby for the first time, as it were.

Alone? Or would Malachi come even after everything she'd said?

She wondered what he was thinking. How he might feel. She'd had three months to get her head around it. And it was growing inside *her* body—she could feel the changes even if she couldn't see them. But Malachi had barely had a week to get used to the idea.

It should have taken her less than ninety seconds to get to the ultrasound unit, yet she dawdled, her eyes darting over every face, the back of every head, as she made her way along the corridor.

The wave of nausea which began to swell inside her had nothing to do with morning sickness.

He really wasn't coming, and it was all her own fault.

the part of a parent? It was why he'd set up Care to Play with his brother. In order to help young carers have some semblance of a childhood in a way that he had never enjoyed. But he never wanted to bear that responsibility himself again.

And yet here he was. In a consultation room with a woman who was little more than a stranger and an unborn baby he would never have chosen to have.

But it was what it was, and he would deal with it the best way he could. The way he dealt with everything in his life…

Malachi didn't know the exact moment he went from detached to awestruck.

Perhaps it was when he saw the image come into focus on the sonographer's screen. Or when he saw the distinct outline of the baby's head. Or maybe it was when he heard the strong, rapid beat of his baby's heart.

He didn't know. And yet in that instant everything…*shifted*. His world began to tilt, slowly at first, then faster. It started to rotate, and spin, and he felt himself toppling, then falling.

His baby.

And Saskia's.

And he knew he would go to the ends of the earth to protect it.

'We should talk…' Saskia bit her lip as they stepped out of the consultation room together.

Gripping the handrail, Saskia stopped in a glass hallway and fought to draw a breath. She'd thought she didn't know what she wanted. Apparently she knew more than she'd realised.

She wanted her baby to have its father.

Not necessarily marriage, as Malachi had put forward, but…*something*. She'd been lying when she'd told him she could do it alone. Lying to him or to herself, she couldn't be sure. Either way, she should have bent a little more. She should have compromised.

But then she'd never been very good at that. It had been one of the many criticisms that Andy had levelled at her which he'd been right about. Of course there was also an argument to say that if Andy had been a fairer, more honest, more loyal fiancé, then perhaps she would have actually *wanted* to compromise more.

Well, it was too late now. She'd made her bed, as they said. Now she had to go and get scanned on it.

Maybe afterwards, if she was feeling brave, she would take a detour past Malachi's apartment. Perhaps even apologise for her curtness last week.

Lifting her head, Saskia focused on moving forward, one step at a time, until she finally reached the end of the corridor and went through the double doors to the booking-in desk.

* * *

'Cutting it a bit fine, aren't you?'

His dry voice in her ear had Saskia spinning in an instant.

'You came!'

She actually seemed pleased to see him there, and for a moment Malachi was thrown.

He'd half expected her to tell him he was not wanted at the scan. He'd even been prepared for it.

Saskia had laid her position out all too clearly the other night, when she'd turned down his marriage proposal without even a hint of a qualm. She didn't need him and she didn't really even want him—at least not outside the bedroom.

But he was the father of her unborn baby, and he had no intention of letting the child grow up thinking he didn't want to be a part of its life. That he didn't care.

He'd gone through the whole gamut of emotions after Saskia had left his apartment a week ago, yet he still didn't know exactly how he felt. He only knew that he was this baby's father and as such he had a responsibility both to it and to Saskia. Whatever she might wish.

And now she was smiling at him as though she was glad he was here. As though she hadn't told him that she could do it alone. As though she hadn't spelled out that he was nothing more than a rebound to her, and that it made no difference

to her whether he was part of their live[s]. As though she hadn't turned on him, dis[missed] his relevance in her life the way his mot[her] done to him—and to Sol—all those year[s].

He'd let his guard down with Saskia.

He wouldn't make that mistake again.

'Don't worry. I'm only here for the baby[—] for you,' he murmured, as he accompanie[d] to the chairs, carrying her file in his hand.

She blinked at him, and something he coul[d] identify flashed through those rich choco[late] depths. Then it was gone.

'Glad to hear it. I wouldn't want to have to tu[rn] down yet another hollow marriage proposal.'

'Trust me, I have no intention of repeatin[g] that.'

There had to be something wrong with him[,] because every single word burned in his throat, acrid and bitter, whilst Saskia offered him a curt bob of the head as though finally—barely—she was satisfied.

Malachi gritted his teeth and waited for her name to be called, unable to stop himself from placing his hand at the small of her back as they walked in, helpless to control this protective instinct that surged inside him when he looked at her.

It made no sense. He'd vowed to himself long ago that a wife, children, weren't for him. Hadn't he sacrificed so much of his childhood to playing

'We should,' he agreed smoothly. 'I think we need to start again.'

She smiled, almost shyly. 'I'd like that.'

Whatever he'd expected her to say, it hadn't been that. But why object when she was only voicing the thoughts in his own head.

'A late lunch?' he suggested, glancing at his watch.

It was the kind of timepiece that cost more than some people's cars. He'd prided himself on that purchase. A reward for his first half a million.

Suddenly it seemed empty.

'I can't.'

Saskia shook her head, and he might even have thought she sounded genuinely disappointed.

'I have to get back to the ward. Technically, I'm in the middle of a full weekend shift.'

'A full weekend?'

Was this her way of giving him the brush-off?

After the scan he'd thought they'd turned a corner.

Had that just been in his head?

'Friday to Monday,' she confirmed. 'We don't get them that often, but when we do it's pretty full-on.'

'Fine. Lunch Tuesday, then. That will give you a day to recover.' It wasn't a question. 'Look after yourself and the baby, and I'll pick you up at midday. I'll take you for lunch.'

'Tuesday.' She nodded, and then she flashed him a smile which seemed to send light cascading right through him.

He really was in trouble.

'Yep, small bowel atresia.' The paediatric surgeon eyed the X-ray with Saskia. 'Good call.'

Good call—crappy outcome, Saskia thought as she considered the newborn baby at the other end of that X-ray.

She had practically floated back to the ward after her scan—and after talking to Malachi—but now everything had crashed back in. Hard. Painful.

The tiny girl they were discussing had only come into the world days before—a little premature, but apparently healthy, if a touch jaundiced, and passing a little meconium. Within hours it had become clear that she was vomiting every time she tried to feed, and the green colour, along with an examination, had revealed a swollen abdomen, leading Saskia to consider a bowel blockage.

She dealt with sick babies and children on a daily basis, but today it was really getting to her.

She fought to pull her head back into the game. 'No contrast scan?' she verified with the surgeon. 'Enema?'

'Not this time. The image is clear enough.'

'Okay…well, she's on a fluid drip now because she was dehydrated,' Saskia confirmed.

'Fine. I'll go and have a chat with the parents. What are they like?'

'Young. Terrified.' Not that she could blame them.

'Right, leave it with me. I'll give them a brief outline now, and once Rosie is stable I'll take them through the operation in more detail.'

'That's great, thanks,' nodded Saskia as her colleague jerked her head to the end of the ward, where children's A&E lay beyond.

'Looks bad out there.'

'Yeah well, typical winter, even more hectic than usual.' Saskia blew out a breath. 'Lots of respiratory—colds, flu—and more kids than we have room for, but I can't possibly send them home.'

'You're under pressure to clear out?'

'All the time.' Saskia grimaced as they headed out of the door, her mind still threatening to wander.

'Well, good luck with it.'

'Yeah, thanks.' She bared her teeth in a semblance of a smile as she passed the board again to check anything new.

That little girl could probably go home.

This guy was waiting for bloods.

That boy could go home.

Still, it barely even scratched the surface.

And now she would have to set up a nasogastric tube to drain off Rosie's stomach and bowel contents, as well as any gas build-up. It wasn't the first time she'd had to prep for an operation on a newborn—not by any stretch—but suddenly the enormity of it hit her.

Being pregnant with her own baby had suddenly brought the reality of the situation home to her. As well as how fragile and precious life was. Maybe marrying Malachi and making sure her child had the best possible start wasn't such a bad plan after all.

She would have security. Support. Someone with whom to share the burden—and the joy. Not to mention the fact that she couldn't do any worse than commit her life to a cheat and liar, which she'd nearly done with Andy.

Somehow she didn't think Malachi was the type to cheat or lie.

And sexual attraction has absolutely nothing to do with it, she concluded, somewhat redundantly.

It was a logical decision. One which had absolutely nothing to do with her libido. All that was left to do now was to tell him.

Suddenly Tuesday lunch with Malachi couldn't come around soon enough.

CHAPTER SEVEN

ELEVEN FORTY-FIVE, SASKIA THOUGHT, checking her watch as she exited her apartment block, her stomach in knots as it had been all weekend, when even the avalanche of a caseload hadn't taken her mind off the scan. And Malachi Gunn.

She probably should have waited upstairs, for fear of looking overkeen for this non-date with Malachi, but she'd been wearing a trench in the living room floor as it was. Better to be out here, waiting in the winter evening, than up there getting cabin fever.

And suddenly there he was. Languishing against the side of a sleek black car which looked as though it belonged on a waiting list as long as the A&E department's patient list on New Year's Eve. And he looked as though he belonged in some designer aftershave advert.

Her heart clattered against her ribs, and it was easier to concentrate on the muscular lines of the car than the muscular lines of the man himself. Confident, self-possessed, and altogether too tempting for words.

He shifted, and this time it was her stomach's turn to give a little lurch.

Hunger pangs, she reprimanded herself sharply. *If only they were.*

'You're early,' she managed, instantly cringing at such a less-than-stellar opening line.

'I might point out the same,' he replied dryly, opening the passenger door and waiting for her to get in. 'I would have preferred to come up to your apartment rather than hover out here like some adolescent waiting for his girlfriend to sneak out of her parents' house.'

Girlfriend? Was that what she was? She tried not to let her body do funny things at his use of the term.

'Funny,' she threw back, as lightly as she could manage, not quite able to move. 'But I'm telling you, my nosy neighbour is worse than any overbearing parents. The grapevine would have been positively shaking before we'd even left the building.'

'Then I suppose it's good that you came down at all.'

There was something in his voice which made her snap her head up. 'Did you think I wouldn't?'

He shot her a masked look which she couldn't quite read. 'I wondered.'

Her curiosity was piqued. 'What would you have done?'

'I'd probably have come up to your door and thrown you over my shoulder and made a scene in front of all your gossiping neighbours.'

'Oh.'

There had to be something wrong with her, she thought, that the idea should appeal so much to some perverse part of her.

'Or perhaps you might have enjoyed that,' Malachi continued quietly, the gleam in his eyes spearing through her right to her core.

She tilted her chin up. 'I most certainly would not.'

He grinned, a devastating smile that she could feel blooming though every inch of her body.

'Then get in the car, or we'll both find out how false that statement is.'

It was as if he had some kind of hold on her. The way her body was moving towards him— *obeying* him—even though her brain was bellowing its objections.

He closed her door and strode around the front of the car, powerful yet graceful, making it impossible for her not to gawk. When he slid into the seat beside her, his thigh too close to hers, and the heat from his body radiated over her, she pretended that a delicious shiver *didn't* dance all the way up her spine. That her chest *didn't* tighten as though he'd sucked all the air from the confined space.

Saskia could feel the pulse at her throat, her wrist, her groin, beating out a frantic SOS. Or perhaps it was tapping out a joyous jig.

If he'd suggested ditching the meal and going straight back to his apartment she knew she wouldn't have objected. Heat suffused her, making her dress feel too scratchy on her skin, her body too tight for itself, her breasts too heavy.

God, she really did need to get a grip.

'You also mentioned that you didn't want your friend to see me.'

His voice dragged her back to the present, getting closer to the heart of the matter. Unease washed through her.

'Yet,' she clarified. 'I don't want her to see you *yet*.'

'Because…?'

'Because I haven't told her I'm pregnant.'

'Maybe you don't think it's any of her business?'

Saskia shook her head slowly. Uncertainly. 'No, we tell each other everything.' *Usually.* 'We've been best friends since we were kids, when our mothers were rivals in the same prime-time American soap opera. We've done everything together—including coming to the UK to become doctors.'

'Yet she doesn't know about the baby? About us?'

'And what do I say about "us"?' Saskia asked, before she could stop herself.

It wasn't exactly the way she'd intended to get to the subject of accepting his marriage proposal, but she supposed it would achieve the same thing.

Instead of replying, however, Malachi simply started the engine, the power of the vehicle humming all around them whilst they pulled away, leaving her fighting to unglue her tongue from the roof of her mouth.

They were speeding along the motorway before she succeeded. He was a good driver, but then, why wouldn't he be? She got the impression that Malachi Gunn was the best at everything he chose to do.

And maybe that wasn't such a bad thing, she considered, since she'd been feeling a little lost ever since she'd found out she was pregnant. Maybe now was the perfect time to tell him everything she'd been reconsidering. Everything she'd spent the past few days practising how to say.

She opened her mouth to speak.

'I apologise for the caveman routine the other week,' he announced unexpectedly.

Her well-rehearsed speech flew out of the window. 'Pardon?'

Something hitched inside Saskia. She couldn't remember Andy apologising for anything, *ever*. Even when he'd been cheating on her. He'd always claimed apologising was a sign of weakness, and she, to her shame, had come to believe him.

Now she realised just how foolish she'd been believing that, too.

It didn't make Malachi look weak at all. Quite the opposite. He looked utterly secure in his own skin. Plus, as she didn't imagine he was a man who often had to apologise, the very fact that he even had made her feel valued. Respected.

'Insisting on marriage,' he was saying as she yanked herself back to the present. 'Being a couple. That was…ill-thought-out.'

Saskia's mouth went dry.

Just as she had decided that it was a good idea.

She should have kept her distance after all— emotionally and physically.

Every fear she'd ever had crashed over her at once. This had to be how it felt to drown.

Saskia tried to rearrange her thoughts, but they jumbled together like a tangle of wires that she couldn't even begin to find the ends of.

'You don't want to be part of our lives after all?' She barely recognised her own voice. It sounded so detached and…*alien*.

'No—there's no question that I will be a part of your lives,' he corrected. 'But you were right to argue that marriage would overcomplicate things. It isn't the solution.'

'I see,' she managed, even though she didn't see at all. 'So what now?'

His momentary silence caught her off guard, and she swivelled her head to find him looking at her. Gauging. Assessing. She tried to relax, for fear of him reading every emotion etched clearly on her face, but she wasn't sure she had succeeded.

Finally he turned back, to concentrate on the road, and she exhaled silently. Hopefully she hadn't given herself away completely, but at least he didn't look entirely at ease himself. If she hadn't known better, she might have thought his set jaw meant he felt as at sea as she did.

She tossed the idea over and over in her mind. On the one hand Malachi wasn't the kind of man she could imagine second-guessing himself. On the other... Well, her gut was telling her he was playing his cards close to his chest. That he still wanted her every bit as much as she wanted him.

'Now,' he echoed firmly, 'we find a solution that works all round. Now we talk.'

'And by *talk* you mean we won't end up in bed this time?'

She was hectoring him. Trying to get a rise out of him. The thing was, she couldn't figure out why. Or, more accurately, she was pretending she couldn't. Either way, Malachi didn't look amused. If anything, he seemed to grimace.

'That won't be happening again, believe me.'

'Right.' She told herself she shouldn't feel hurt by his wintry tone. 'Good to know.'

Was he trying to convince her, or himself? Could he turn off his attraction just like that? Because there was no way she was able to do it.

They lapsed into another edgy silence.

Saskia tried to concentrate on the drive, but all she could think about was the fact that only a few months ago Malachi had given her the most intimate, passionate weekend of her life—which was vaguely sad in itself, given how many years she'd been engaged to Andy—and there hadn't been one single uncomfortable moment between the two of them. Yet now they were walking on eggshells around each other.

Eventually, she couldn't stand it any longer. 'So where are we going, then?'

'I thought I might take you somewhere civilised.'

'Civilised?'

She feared she liked the sound of that far more than she should.

'A restaurant.'

'Like…a date?' It was out before she could stop it.

He cast her another impenetrable look. 'More

like somewhere we can talk. Somewhere neutral.'

'Out of the city?' she noted.

And not at his apartment.

Who was it he didn't trust? Her? Or himself? She suspected it was sadly the former.

He didn't answer immediately. Instead he pulled off the road and onto a small Tarmac clearing.

A helicopter stood a hundred or so metres away.

'You could say it's out of the city...'

'That's for us?' Saskia schooled her features, ignoring the goosebumps that travelled up her arms.

'It is.'

'And that's the pilot?' She glanced at the man sitting in a car on the other side of the Tarmac.

'No, that's Bill. He's just been looking after the heli for me.'

Her stomach flip-flopped in anticipation.

'Let me guess—you're the pilot.'

Malachi lifted one easy shoulder, then set about helping her up into the passenger seat.

'Trust me...' he murmured.

The startling thing was that she did.

She couldn't help but thrill at it all, even as she knew she was being ridiculous. And part of her whispered that he seemed to be going to a lot of effort for someone he no longer wanted to marry.

The smarting she'd felt earlier eased a little.

Which only served to panic her all the more.

Frantically, she tried to remind herself that Malachi was all about practicality. She told herself that he'd probably chosen the helicopter so she couldn't keep wittering in his ear, the way she had in the car. She instructed herself that there was nothing romantic about this moment.

Nothing at all.

It was a shame her body—and her soaring heart—didn't want to agree. All they wanted to do was revel in the fact that he wasn't walking away from her and their baby after all.

'When I said "out of the city" you didn't tell me you meant out of the country!'

Saskia savoured another delicious mouthful of the sumptuous winterberry soufflé—the final course of her two-Michelin-star meal.

The day had been surprisingly pleasant, given their conversation a few hours earlier in the car. At some point over the English Channel, they had clearly decided that the frosty atmosphere wasn't going to help the situation, so by the time Malachi had landed the helicopter they'd both been trying hard to lighten the mood.

She had to admit that the incredible venue had significantly helped matters.

'I've dreamed of visiting France, and this restaurant, for years.'

'I remember,' he told her, his eyes holding hers without wavering. 'You saw it in a magazine that weekend we were together, and told me you'd heard of this place when you first moved to the UK. You said that you and Anouk had always talked about visiting it.'

'You remember that?' She stared at him.

'I do.'

She cocked her head to one side. 'Well, I also remember reading that it's always booked up months and months in advance.'

'An opening became available.'

He shrugged it off but she wasn't fooled.

He'd done all this for her. This definitely wasn't a way of brushing her or the baby off. Relief, and another emotion, uncoiled within her.

'I thought it would be nice for us to talk somewhere like this. Besides, you seem to be enjoying the menu.'

Saskia smoothed the frown from her face before it could take hold properly.

'Is that a backhanded compliment?' She forced a lightness into her tone, as if the words didn't really bother her. 'I suppose I could pretend to be one of those people who push lettuce leaves around their plate and claim not to be hungry, but I'm afraid that has never been me.'

'I can't imagine you ever pretending to be anything you aren't.'

He'd surprised her by saying that. And it sent

a warm glow through her even as she schooled herself not to react.

'But, for the record, it was a straightforward compliment.'

The glow intensified. 'Good to know…' She had no idea how she managed to sound nonchalant.

'Still, I didn't bring you here to bandy about compliments. I brought you because I want to start over. Talk about our baby.'

'And you want to be part of our lives?' she asked carefully, not wanting him to realise she needed more reassurance right now.

'I believe I said that earlier.' He frowned. 'I'm trying to be understanding here. To bend a little. And believe me, *zvyozdochka*, I am not a man accustomed to having to bend. I suggest you don't take it as a sign that you can try to exclude me from any decisions pertaining to our baby.'

Relief punched through her. And a little bit of her old fighting spirit.

Andy had crushed it by his betrayal, but it appeared as though her each and every encounter with Malachi went some way to restoring it. As if he was somehow…*good* for her.

'I wasn't going to exclude you from anything,' she managed haughtily, in an effort not to let him see what she was really feeling. 'But if you're no longer insisting on marriage, how exactly do you envisage things between us working out?'

* * *

How indeed? Malachi wondered, and not for the first time.

In truth, he hadn't got that far in his plan. For a man who usually approached business ventures like a chess game, always making sure he was several moves ahead, he was astonishingly poorly prepared when it came to Saskia and his baby.

It was as though the moment she entered into any thought process he couldn't even see straight, let alone plan straight.

It was frustrating, thrilling, and terrifying all at the same time.

Moreover, her haughty tone seemed to work its way through him like a stormproof match in a state-of-the-art survival kit. Even if she submerged him in the coldest hauteur he was afraid he would still blaze brightly for her.

Which was exactly why marriage to her had been a reckless idea.

He was altogether too afraid that having her under his roof, that sinful body of hers within arm's reach, and knowing exactly how wickedly she melted into him, he wouldn't be able to stay on task.

Even now he wanted to touch her, taste her again. It was one of the reasons he'd chosen to fly her out of the country, well away from the temptation of taking her back to his apartment.

His one priority right now had to be their baby, and after the scan the other day he knew it wasn't going to be as impossible as he'd feared.

Even at the memory of that ultrasound Malachi felt his chest tighten. His heart stopped, then restarted with a lurch.

His baby. *Their* baby.

So impossibly, exquisitely perfect.

Seeing his baby moving on that screen and hearing its heartbeat hadn't just unlocked the cage on his long-restrained heart—it had smashed it apart and splintered it into a million worthless pieces.

His entire chest felt full. Bursting. And the baby wasn't even born yet. How the hell was he going to cope when it was cradled in his arms?

He had known in that moment that he would protect it with his life. And Saskia, too, of course, as the mother of his child. But marrying her wasn't the way to do that. Not least because being around her made him feel wholly and completely out of control.

It all led to a conundrum he was more than happy not to answer. For Saskia, however, it seemed to be the only question she wanted answered.

'Do you intend for me to live out of a suitcase—some nights of the week at your apartment and some nights at my own?' she asked. 'Or perhaps you propose to come and spend some nights at the apartment Anouk and I share?'

'There is an apartment available in my building. I thought you could move in there. That way we would still have our own space, but our baby would have both its parents around all the time.'

It might not exactly be a stroke of genius, but Malachi was more than happy that it was a fair halfway meeting.

Saskia looked disgruntled. 'Are you serious?'

'You have an objection?' he managed mildly.

'Well...yes!' she seethed. 'You're talking about installing me in an apartment in your building like some kind of mistress you're moving in for your convenience.'

'I was thinking about what makes sense for you and the baby.' He narrowed his gaze. 'But I find it interesting that you should use the term *mistress*. Are you making me a proposition?'

'I most certainly am not,' she returned.

But he noted the dark colour staining her cheeks and her long, elegant neck, and could only imagine just how far it spread down her lush body.

'Your body language might suggest otherwise.'

'Then learn to read it better,' she snapped.

He tried to suppress the urge to grin, but it was too strong. It was this damn spell that Saskia kept putting him under. The idea was that he was supposed to be taking control of this situation, not falling for her charms like some little lapdog.

'That sounds like another invitation,' he drawled. 'A pity that I have to decline.'

'It wasn't an invitation.' She jutted her chin out obstinately. 'And even if it was, I don't believe you would decline. I remember how your body responds to me, Malachi. I know I'm not the only one who was lost in the moment the other night.'

'You're remembering what you want to remember, *zvyozdochka*. My advice to you is to stop fighting me and to remember that we're on the same team.'

'Yes—because it's so easy to feel that way when you're commanding me to upend my life and move away from my support system just to make things easier for you.'

He hated it that her dismissal of his role in her life stung as it did.

'Do I have to remind you, yet again, that you are carrying *my* child? I am your support system. From now on we are one unit.'

'One unit even though you no longer wish to marry me?' she threw back at him. 'One unit even though you don't even want to share your home with me?'

The problem with that, of course, was that he *did* want to share his home with her. And his bed. Possibly far too much.

'Careful, *zvyozdochka*, or I might believe that

you're actually pining for that option. That you were anticipating sharing your life with me with pleasure, despite all your earlier objections.'

'You can't really believe that!' She laughed.

It was a brittle little sound that revealed things he imagined she had never wanted him to know. Not least that he was right.

Lust fired through him like a slingshot, right around his sex.

'I've told you how things are going to be. For both you and our child,' he growled.

The temptation to take her hand and lead her from this restaurant to an exclusive hotel he knew was right around the corner was almost overwhelming.

'And you've said it—ergo that is how it will be?' she retorted.

He made an approving click of his tongue, which was guaranteed to get her back up all the more.

It was either that or stir an altogether different emotion in her.

In both of them.

'And now, *zvyozdochka*, I suggest we get back to the helicopter. We have a long flight home.'

'Good,' she muttered. 'Because I'm sure I could do with the thinking time.'

CHAPTER EIGHT

'WHAT'S HAPPENED?' SASKIA yelled over the rotor blades as she raced across Moorlands General's helipad.

The call had come in just as they'd been twenty minutes out. A major incident in the area—some kind of explosion, from what Saskia could gather—meant that all available staff were being called in to the hospital.

Malachi hadn't even needed to ask her. He'd instinctively turned his helicopter, calling in a new flight plan and instructing his PA to check that there were no air ambulances in the area before getting permission for him to land at the hospital with Saskia.

'Some kind of gas explosion on Beechmoor Street!' her colleague shouted. 'Near the junction with King's Boulevard. There are multiple casualties and they're splitting them between us and the Royal.'

'Where do you want me?'

'There's a designated area for incident victims

in paediatric A&E. Fortunately because of the time of day, there weren't too many kids around, and those that were appear to have been caught more by the shockwaves than in the blast itself.'

'Thank goodness. Listen, do you know if Anouk—Dr Hart—is okay?'

'I don't know, sorry. Apparently the area has been evacuated.'

Biting her lip, Saskia hurried down the ramp and into the hospital. Behind her she could hear Malachi's helicopter leaving, but she didn't turn around. There wasn't time.

'Come on, then. Let's go.'

Saskia glanced at the screen as her colleague ran her through the latest admissions.

'First up is five-year-old Molly, who was knocked into a wall during the explosion and suffered a head injury. She was Emily's patient, but Em's now tied up with someone else. Molly has already been to CT and everything is clear— she just needs stitches.'

'Okay, great.' Saskia nodded. 'Let me go and see her and check the injury, and then I'll get some kit together.'

The place was heaving, and her colleagues were triaging new admissions as fast as they came in. The beds were filling up fast. The sooner they could clear the non-urgent patients out, the better.

'Hi, I'm Saskia.' She smiled as she stepped

around the curtain. 'I'll be the doctor looking after you. You must be Molly.'

'I am,' the little girl said proudly, returning her smile with a happy, confident one of her own. 'And this is my mummy.'

'Hello, Mummy,' Saskia said dutifully.

'Hi.' The young woman shot her a relieved smile, the hint of tension around her eyes belying her calm exterior.

'Right, I know you've been through this with the other doctor—'

'Dr Emily,' the girl interjected.

'Right...'

'She's nice.'

'Yes, she is,' Saskia agreed.

Clearly there was no impairment in Molly's speech or understanding, which was a good sign. But although the little girl had already been checked over, another set of eyes never hurt.

'I think you seem nice, too.'

'Thank you.' Saskia laughed. 'I'm glad you think so. Anyway, I know you've told the other doctor what happened, but can you tell me, too?'

'Of course I can!' the little girl exclaimed with an expansive gesture. 'Mummy and I were out shopping for some new shoes.'

'Oh, lovely,' Saskia offered, when it appeared the five-year-old was waiting for a reply.

Clearly, it wasn't the response Molly was hoping for.

'Red *patent leather* shoes,' she emphasised after a moment.

'Wow,' Saskia managed, relieved when the little girl nodded with satisfaction.

'And when we got them we called in to see Nana, and she thought they were *bee-yoo-tiful.*'

'Well, of course,' agreed Saskia solemnly. 'But I'd really love it if you could tell me some more about how you hit your head.'

'Oh…' The girl's face fell. Clearly to her the red patent leather shoes were the most important detail of her experience.

Saskia stifled a chuckle.

'I don't really remember. We were walking back, and suddenly there was a really, really loud bang, and then I was on the other side of the pavement and my head was bleeding.'

'Did it hurt?'

'Yes. A *lot.*'

'Can I see?' Saskia stood up and Molly obligingly turned around.

'Of course.'

Tentatively she parted the matted hair and checked the wound. It had evidently been cleaned once, so it was easy to see what was going on.

'Great. And can you remember how you got here, Molly?'

'Mummy brought me in.'

'We were right around the corner,' the mother put in. 'The traffic was heavy, and I knew I could get her here before an ambulance even got out. I didn't even think about head or neck injuries. I know I should have.'

'It's okay,' soothed Saskia. 'I just wanted to see if Molly remembered what had happened and how she felt.'

'I was told the CT scan was fine?'

'It is. Please don't worry. I just wanted to check once more for good measure. Right, Molly, let me go and get my equipment, and then I'm going to give you just a little injection in the back of your head to make sure you don't feel anything—okay?'

'Okay.' Molly nodded cheerfully.

Confident about her patient, Saskia headed out of the bay for a couple of suture kits and some local anaesthetic, glad the little girl didn't seem in any distress, either physically or emotionally.

She was on her way back to the bay when she saw Anouk dashing past the doors at the end of the ward, flanked by two porters pushing a gurney. Relief washed over her. At least her friend was all right. But it didn't look as though they were going to get chance to talk any time soon.

'Right, here we are,' she popped back through the curtain. 'Mum, can you sit here for me? And, Molly, can you lie face down on the bed, looking at your mummy? Good girl.'

Quickly and efficiently she began cleaning the

area, and then carefully administered the anaesthetic.

'You might feel a bit of a sharp sting, but then it should feel better. If you can keep as still as you can, sweetheart? Wow, good girl—that was brilliant.'

'Mummy says I'm very brave,' Molly said proudly.

'Mummy is right.'

She distracted the girl for a few moments longer whilst the anaesthetic took hold.

'Okay, this shouldn't hurt, but if you feel any pinching at all you let me know—all right, Molly?'

'All right.'

Working speedily, Saskia began her sutures, twelve in all, and they were made easier by the fact that the five-year-old kept still and focused on her mum, who chatted to her quietly throughout about Nana and the red shoes.

Would she be as calm and collected if it was her child?

She could imagine Malachi being so. It was a nice feeling. But she told herself it was probably just hormones.

'Okay, Molly, we're all done,' she declared as she finished up. 'You were amazing.'

'Good enough for jelly sweets, Mummy?'

'I think maybe you were.' The young woman bent down to kiss her daughter tenderly.

'Right, just rest here while I go and fill in the

discharge forms.' Saskia smiled, piling the detritus back into the cardboard bowl and slipping off her gloves.

Just a little longer, to check Molly was okay, and then they could leave. With a final word of congratulation to the brave girl, Saskia slipped out of the bay and back to the desk, to bring the case up on the screen.

Her colleague was on her within moments.

'When you've finished that one, Saskia, there's a nine-year-old in Bay Twelve, complaining of shoulder and back pain. Also caught in the explosion.'

'No problem,' Saskia confirmed.

It looked as if it was going to be a long night.

It was twenty-four hours before the last of the major incident casualties were cleared, either to various departments or home. There were a few stragglers with non-life-threatening injuries still left to be brought in by road, but most of the air ambulances had stopped bringing in critical cases a while ago. The road ambulance arrivals—along with the usual A&E walk-ins— could be dealt with by the new shift.

Her work was done, and Saskia was more relieved than she cared to admit.

Because the pains that had started in her abdomen earlier were still there. Still worrying her.

Her mobile pinged just as she was heading into the locker room to collect her clothes.

Malachi.

The urge to hear his voice suddenly overwhelmed her. Before she could talk herself out of it she swiped the screen and let her phone dial his number.

He picked it up almost instantly. 'Saskia?'

She stopped in the corridor, staring at her phone as her brain sifted through a dozen things to say, whilst her voice couldn't articulate a single one of them.

'Is everything all right, *zvyozdochka*?'

She bit her lip. What was she even doing, calling him?

'Saskia?' he barked into the silent line, almost making her jump into action.

'I'm here.'

'Are you all right?'

'No, I don't think so. I'm not sure.'

'I'm coming in.'

'I... No... Listen, I...' She was stalling.

'I'm coming in,' he repeated. 'Don't leave without me. Is the incident over?'

'It seems to be.'

'Then I'll bring the heli in again. There's so much debris out there the city will still be gridlocked. Besides, it's getting late and the air ambulance pilots will need to get the copters back to base before it goes dark. I'm closer. I can afford to fly that little bit later.'

She should say no. She shouldn't have even called him. They weren't a couple, as he'd pointed out earlier. Or had it been the day before? Her brain faltered. The emergency had gone on so long and time seemed to have merged into itself. She was so tired. Exhausted.

'Okay, I'll head up to the roof now.'

She glanced at the door to the bathroom. *Right after she checked that her worst fears hadn't come true.*

She was just changing her shoes when Anouk rounded the corner, walking straight into her. Without a word she stepped forward and hugged her tightly.

'I was so relieved when I heard you were safe.'

'Why wouldn't I be?' Anouk laughed. 'And never mind me—the hospital is practically buzzing with some gossip that you arrived by private helicopter?'

Saskia thrust her away, her eyes searching Anouk's. 'You haven't heard, then?' she demanded.

'Heard what?'

'That the explosion affected King's Boulevard?'

'That's us.' Anouk frowned.

'Yes. The whole area has been cordoned off until they can determine which buildings are structurally intact and which aren't. We can't go home.'

Anouk didn't answer and Saskia hugged her again. Though whether it was to make her friend feel better or herself, she couldn't quite be sure.

'At least we're both safe.'

'We should book a hotel, then…' Anouk looked dazed. 'I'll call now.'

Guilt jostled around Saskia's chest.

'Not for me.' She placed her hand over Anouk's to still her, even as she reached into her locker for her mobile. 'I'm… I have somewhere to be.'

'Where?'

The guilt swelled. And with it another sharp abdominal pain. It took everything she had not to wince. Not to let Anouk see. Not until she knew what was going on with her body, and not until she'd told Malachi first.

'I… I'm staying with Malachi,' she managed.

'With Malachi?'

Anouk frowned, peering at her a little too closely for Saskia's peace of mind. And then the unmistakable baritone of Sol Gunn, top neurosurgeon and Malachi's brother, came to her rescue.

'Saskia? Are you in here?'

And then he appeared in person, and all Saskia could wonder was whether he knew about her and his brother. If so, how *much* did he know?

But when he rounded the corner fully, his attention seemed distracted.

'Oh, Anouk…'

He paused for a fraction of a second before turning back to her. *Curious.*

'Mal says you need to get going, Saskia. His heli is on the roof and they want it cleared in case another emergency has to come in.'

'I'm going,' Saskia muttered, but Sol had already turned back to her friend, an intense expression clouding his face.

'If you're calling for a hotel, Anouk, you're too late. I heard a couple of guys complaining an hour ago that every hotel in the city is booked out. The cordon is quite extensive—lots of apartment blocks have been evacuated.'

'Great.'

Anouk gritted her teeth and Saskia couldn't bring herself to leave. If their apartment block was in the cordon then Anouk would have nowhere to go. Yet she could hardly invite her back to Malachi's; she didn't even know where she stood with him herself.

'You could find an on-call room,' she suggested hesitantly.

'I'm guessing they'll all be taken, too,' Sol told them. 'They're setting up temporary beds in community centres all around the place.'

'Oh…' Anouk's face fell, and Saskia couldn't help grabbing her friend's hand.

'I could speak to Malachi? See if you can come with us?'

'Or you could just stay with me,' Sol cut in quietly, firmly.

He didn't add to the sentence, but it hung there in the silence. Slowly, so slowly, the reason for the tension between Sol and Anouk dawned on her.

Could it really be…?

'Thanks,' Anouk managed stiffly, 'but I don't think it's a good idea.'

It was just too deliciously ironic to be true. Her and Malachi? Anouk and Sol?

'That's a great idea,' Saskia gushed, before Anouk could shut him down.

When was the last time Anouk had done anything crazy? Why not now?

'I'm sorry—I do have to go,' she muttered, squeezing Anouk's hand again, as if that could convey all the things she couldn't say to her friend in front of Sol.

'I don't understand, Sask?'

She wished, not for the first time, that she'd found a way to tell her friend about the baby. But this wasn't the time.

'It's complicated. I'll explain everything when I can.'

Then Saskia hurried out of the room, before she could say anything more to give herself away.

The cramps were stronger now, along with

chest pain. Gripping the wall, Saskia made her way down the corridor and into the bathroom. She needed to know if she was losing the baby.

Slipping into the stall, she closed her eyes and sent a silent plea out into the ether.

No blood. Not even spotting. No sign that she was losing her baby. Thank goodness.

Saskia slumped against the wall with relief. A sob racked her. It was incredible that something she hadn't even thought about, let alone planned, should mean so much to her, and yet it did.

Which was why she needed to go to the maternity wing now, and make sure everything was all right.

Whatever the situation with Malachi, she wasn't going to shut him out of their lives. This was his baby, too, and whether he chose to be a part of it or not would have to be his choice. They were never going to have the kind of deep, passionate love her parents had shared, but that could only be a good thing when she thought about how they had ended up devastating her as a child. She should be pleased that Malachi wanted to be an active part of his child's life.

It was wrong to want to keep him at bay simply because she didn't think she could handle their physical attraction. Which meant that right now he had as much right to know what was happening with this pregnancy as she did.

Sucking in a deep breath, Saskia took her mobile out of her bag and, with shaking fingers, texted his number.

Malachi raced down the stairs to the maternity wing and battled not to let his world fall apart all around him.

How was it that a baby he hadn't even thought he wanted a few weeks ago was now the most important thing in his life?

He snatched open the door to the floor and glanced up and down the corridor, trying to find his bearings. *There.* Room 214… Room 216… He kept moving until he found the room number Saskia had texted him, knocked once and walked inside.

She was there alone, a bottle of water gripped with white-knuckle tightness.

'What's going on?' he demanded without preamble.

'Where's your helicopter?' She shot him a shocked, slightly dazed glance, peering around him as though she half expected it to be in the corridor behind him.

'Dealt with.' He just about swallowed his frustration. 'What's happening with you?'

She didn't look as though she'd heard him.

'You can't leave it on the roof. What if an emergency comes in and an air ambulance needs to land?'

'I didn't leave it on the helipad—it's dealt with. It's safe,' he managed. 'Now, tell me about *you*, Saskia.'

'Oh…she's gone to set up a scan,' Saskia blurted, sending his heart tumbling in a fast, wild freefall which he didn't think would ever end. 'Hence the water.'

Of course.

'Is something wrong with the baby?'

'No…maybe…probably not.' She struggled to speak. 'They think I was just having a panic attack. I had abdominal pains, chest pains, some trembling.'

'You have a stressful career and you just worked a major incident after a three-day shift,' he pointed out, trying to keep any hint of accusation out of his voice.

This wasn't about laying blame. It was about understanding what had happened to Saskia, and potentially to their baby, and why.

'Which is why they want to do the scan. Impact on the developing foetus isn't inevitable, but high anxiety could lead to reduced blood flow to the baby, which could result in low birth weight or premature labour.'

The words pounded down on him.

'Premature labour? That can't happen. So from now on do you need bed rest?' he demanded.

'Not bed rest, exactly,' she countered. 'But they may suggest some activity restrictions.'

A low sound rumbled in his chest. 'I need more than that, *zvyozdochka*. Tell me precisely what restrictions.'

'It's not definite yet,' she hedged.

'Saskia.'

The warning was clear, but still she blinked at him before capitulating.

'Fine. Light exercise is fine, but lifting heavy weights, housework, for the moment they're off limits.'

'Work?' he pushed.

'Let's see what the scan shows,' she countered shakily.

He knew he should let it go and give her some semblance of feeling that she was still in control.

But he couldn't.

'I can't imagine they left that open to interpretation when, as a doctor, you're constantly running around a hospital—a highly stressful environment.'

'Lots of pregnant women work.' She narrowed her eyes at him. 'Some even work in hospitals.'

'And they don't end up here,' he said trying to keep the dark, terrible thoughts at bay. 'Afraid for their baby.'

'We don't know anything yet,' Saskia repeated, but there was no strength to her words. Only thinly veiled fear. 'I can't just take the next five months off for a panic attack.'

He softened his voice, taking her hand. 'This

is about the baby. *Our* baby. And your health. If it's about the money, I can cover any expenses.'

'It isn't about the money!' she cried, but she didn't try to pull her hand away. 'This is about letting down the hospital, my patients, my colleagues.'

A savage fury swept through him in that moment, but he couldn't reply. He couldn't even speak.

And then suddenly she shot him a desperate look.

'I don't even know if anything is wrong.'

It was like a fog lifting.

'You feel responsible for them,' he realised abruptly. It was a sensation that he knew only too well, and she didn't need him judging her or condemning her. She needed him to understand and take control.

'I...yes.'

'But this isn't about them. It's about you and it's about our child. And you won't be going through this alone.' Malachi dropped his voice. 'I *will* look after you, *zvyozdochka*.'

She dragged her eyes up to him, searching, imploring. And then she stopped and offered the briefest of nods, her fingers gripping his hand tightly, as though she was never going to let it go.

There was so much more to say. So many ways to reassure her. But at that moment Saskia's consultant returned and, after a brief introduction, led them to an available ultrasound room.

The same one they'd been in for that first scan. It almost felt like fate—if Malachi had ever believed in such things.

But this time the screen was kept turned away from him and Saskia as the checks were carried out, and when Saskia slid her hand back into his all he could do was hold on tightly.

He had no idea what to do with this ball of emotion churning inside him. So he just sat there and stared at the back of the screen, as if he could make everything all right just by sheer force of will.

When the consultant finally glanced up, the faintest smile on her lips, and clicked the sound on so that the baby's rapid constant heartbeat filled the room, it was as if a weight had been lifted.

Still, it felt like an age whilst the rest of the checks were conducted, and he had to sit there, feeling powerless and furious, whilst she prodded Saskia and asked her to move position several times. It felt like another eternity while they took measurements and checked organs.

He'd spent half his life learning to read people, honing the skill to perfection. But right now he couldn't read the consultant's neutral expression, and a part of him didn't even want to. The fact that there wasn't another smile, or any moment of engagement, told him everything.

All he could do was keep Saskia's cold hand nestled in his. The impending news was almost suffocating him, and nightmare scenarios were racing through his mind. He could only imagine the plethora of things that Saskia—a medical professional herself—could be imagining.

'So, the baby looks generally healthy, and it's growing,' the consultant began, showing them a couple of images she'd saved. 'However, there are a couple of areas of concern. The scan shows a potential clubbed foot—but, more concerning, it seems there is a mass on your baby's left foot and another smaller one on the left hand. Your baby's movements seemed to be a little restricted, however, I'd like to do some more rigorous scans before I draw any conclusions——'

'But it's consistent with ABS?' Saskia cut in. 'One professional to another?'

'I'm sorry, Saskia, but it's a working theory, yes.'

Malachi waited for them to elaborate, and when they didn't he spoke.

'ABS?'

'Amniotic Band Syndrome,' Saskia answered dully.

The consultant chimed in quickly. 'But we won't know for sure until we can get some clearer scans.'

'When will that be?' he demanded.

'There's another machine, a better one, but it's in use now. We could try in about half an hour,' she suggested. 'I just need you to keep drinking water, Saskia. That should help, too.'

Saskia grunted in what might have passed as acknowledgement. It only made him feel all the more helpless. There was nothing he could say or do to help right now, and he wasn't used to *not* being the person in the room people looked to in order to solve a problem.

Hell, he didn't know if *anyone* could solve this one.

CHAPTER NINE

'SO IT'S DEFINITELY this Amniotic Band Syndrome?' Malachi gritted out, and Saskia turned
to face him.

If she was feeling this numb, this out of her
own body, then how must Malachi be feeling
right now?

'Can you see those weblike lines on the
image?' she managed jerkily.

'I'm the only non-doctor in this room,' he said
pointedly.

'Right. Sorry. Yes…' her consultant cut in.
'Because it's Saskia, I forgot that you might not
be following. So, ABS is caused by thin strands
of the amniotic sac which have separated and are
wrapping around parts of the baby.'

'But it's a fluid?' he frowned. 'Amniotic fluid.
It's meant to *protect* the baby.'

Saskia shook her head, unable to speak. She'd
had to pass bad news on to parents and guard-
ians countless times, keeping level-headed in
some incredibly high-pressure situations. But

this time she was on the other side of the fence. She couldn't even begin to think straight, let alone make her voice form the words to explain.

'Think of it this way,' the consultant interjected gently. 'Two membranes form around the embryo to protect it during gestation, the amnion and the chorion—almost like one balloon being blown up inside another. In between the two is a sticky substance which allows these two membranes to fuse together, usually by week fourteen.'

'But in this case they haven't,' he stated flatly.

'Right—and sections of the amnion have broken away in long, fine strands. These strands can wrap around the foetus, entangling digits, limbs or other parts of the developing baby.'

'We're at seventeen weeks. Why wasn't this spotted earlier?' he demanded, and Saskia could read the fear and frustration in his voice.

It echoed her own.

She reached out her arm stiffly to touch his.

'The strands are so fine that they can be hard to spot on ultrasound, Malachi,' she whispered. 'A diagnosis is usually made by observing the birth defects caused by ABS.'

He turned his head to look at her, and for a moment they didn't feel like two strangers who had made a baby during a one-night stand. They felt like a unit. A team.

'Like these masses on the baby's left hand and foot?'

'Yes,' the consultant confirmed. 'And the club foot we've seen today.

Malachi turned back to face the woman, away from Saskia. There was no need for Saskia to feel the loss so acutely. Yet she did.

'We…we were intimate,' he bit out at length. 'Last week…'

'No,' the woman shook her head firmly. 'We don't always know what causes chorioamniotic separation, but usually—that is, in about eighty-five percent of cases—it is invasive foetal surgery. Either way, it won't have been sexual intimacy.'

He still looked rigid, as if he wasn't convinced that he wasn't somehow to blame. Saskia wanted to say something but she didn't know what. She didn't know how.

'So what now?' he demanded abruptly.

Something surged through Saskia. She couldn't have said what it was, but it lent her strength suddenly.

'I want surgery.'

'That's what I would advise,' the consultant agreed. 'Though we need to discuss the risks.'

'I know the risks.'

Galvanised, Saskia leaned forward, as though that would somehow better convey her desire.

'But, depending on how tightly those bands

are wrapped around my baby's foot and hand, they could end up amputating them in the womb.'

'So they are going to perform the surgery on you *now*?' Malachi growled. 'I realise this is something you can do—operate on babies in the womb—but this is *my* baby. *Our* baby. Talk me through it. I need to understand.'

'There was something else I noted on the scans which we need to discuss,' the consultant said.

Saskia blinked. 'Something else?'

'At one point during the scan your baby moved. It appeared as though part of it moved out of the amniotic cavity.'

'PROM?' She echoed in disbelief, staring at the consultant.

'Right...'

'What is PROM?' he demanded.

Almost robotically, Saskia turned to face Malachi. 'Premature rupture of the membranes. It means that a purely fetoscopic release of the amniotic bands will be impossible.'

'However, we do have the option of surgery in a CO_2-filled uterus,' the consultant added quickly. 'A laparotomy with fetoscopic release of the bands, along with a partial amnionectomy, likely through two uterine ports, with CO_2 as distention.'

'So you'll cut the bands, remove them from the baby's limbs, then what?' she asked.

'We'll cut them away and remove them from your uterus, as well as any amnion.'

'What about Saskia and the baby?' Malachi cut in. 'How do you monitor them to make sure they're both okay?'

'Normal cardiac function for Saskia will be monitored by heart rate, mitral regurgitation and motion of the heart.' The consultant smiled encouragingly. 'The baby's cardiac function will be intermittently monitored by a separate paediatric cardiologist, using an ultrasound probe placed directly into the uterus to produce an image of the baby's heart.'

'And once the surgery is complete?' Saskia asked.

'We'll remove the gas and replace it with warmed saline, remove the ports and suture the uterine openings. Then, once we've returned the uterus to the abdomen, we'll close up.'

'When will I be able to take her home?' Malachi cut in, and the concern in his voice touched her.

'We won't know until we do the scan,' her colleague advised.

'But what are the possibilities?' he pushed.

'It could be anything from a couple of days to bed rest and a hospital stay for the remainder of the pregnancy—we just don't know. But so long as the recovery is smooth you should be discharged within seventy-two hours—although we'll want to do follow-up scans on a weekly basis.'

'Right…' Saskia managed weakly, and her colleague excused herself to confirm the soonest slot for surgery.

She could live with that. She could live with anything so long as it meant that her baby was going to be all right.

'We will get through this.' Malachi pulled her to him as they sat alone in the room. 'Us and our baby.'

She leaned gratefully against his chest, letting the warmth of his body radiate strength into her and breathing in the woodsy scent that was essentially Malachi.

'Thank you,' she whispered.

'For what?'

'For being here. For…caring.'

His hands moved to her shoulders and he drew her away so he could look at her. 'Did you expect anything less, *zvyozdochka*? It is my baby, too.'

'I know,' she acknowledged. 'And I'm sorry if you thought I was trying to exclude you. I suppose I just wanted what…what my parents had, without allowing for the fact that we are different. Our circumstances are different.'

'I can't give you what you want,' he murmured. 'You want a dramatic, passionate marriage like your parents', but…that isn't who I am.'

'I know,' she began, but then the words stopped in her throat.

Did she know that? Really?

She'd thought she'd known. Only the longer she was with Malachi and the more she saw of his kindness, the more she was beginning to question her childhood. Or, at least, the version that was in her head. She talked about their *great love affair* as if that somehow explained their actions, and how it had ultimately impacted on her—the daughter they were meant to have loved.

Yet now—because of Malachi—she was forced to consider what love really looked like. Volatile, passionate, but ultimately destructive, as they had been? Or was Malachi's quiet, strong steadfastness how love should really look?

But for his child, that baby that she was carrying, she reminded herself hastily. *Not for her.* She couldn't afford to forget that distinction.

'It *will* be who you are. One day. When you find the right person,' she told him softly, swallowing hard and forcing an upbeat tone to try and keep the regret out of her voice. 'Clearly that person isn't me, but no matter what you will be welcome in your child's life. I will never stop you being a part of that. We'll work out a system that works for both for us, and for the baby.'

She'd thought it was the right thing to say. The balanced thing. But Malachi stiffened against her, placing his hands at her shoulders and pulling her from him.

'Am I to thank you for your benevolence?'

His voice abraded her skin. She could feel his repressed anger through every hair follicle on her arms and neck. But she still didn't know what she'd said wrong.

'Even now, through all of this, you're trying to square everything away. Tying me up like some kind of loose end.'

'That's not what I'm doing,' she denied.

'Oh, yes, *zvyozdochka*, that's exactly what you're doing,' he seethed. 'You're frightened about handing over the fate of this baby to the surgeons—your colleagues—so you're trying to control everything else instead.'

'No...' She shook her head, but she couldn't deny that he had introduced an element of doubt.

Hadn't Anouk always teased her for being a micro-manager? And Andy had been less forgiving, calling her a control freak, and a couple of other less palatable names.

'But I warn you that I won't be boxed away like that,' Malachi continued. 'And if you try you will soon find the terms I am capable of exacting in response.'

'What kind of terms?' she asked, despite herself.

'You don't want to know,' he said ominously.

She ought to feel afraid. Instead she felt something else. *Exhilaration?*

'Actually, I rather think I do.' She lifted her head boldly, her gaze colliding with his and holding it.

The tension stretched between them.

'Not now,' he said abruptly.

But she shook her head. 'Precisely now.'

His black look would have had any number of other people—male and female—cowering, but suddenly Saskia realised that she didn't feel intimidated or afraid when it came to Malachi. She never had.

She'd thought it was only a physical attraction they shared, but the truth was that she'd always felt safe with this man. Secure. Especially now.

The revelation knocked the air from her lungs. *So what did that even mean?*

But then there was no time to ponder it, because he was speaking, and it occurred to her that he was doing what she'd asked and telling her what she'd wanted to know.

'Our baby is fragile. Too fragile to be put at any more risk than necessary.'

'I know…' She murmured her agreement.

'And, whilst I understand you love your career as a doctor, there is no way I can believe this high-pressure environment is going to be good for this pregnancy.'

She knew that, too. She'd been thinking about

little else since those first pains had started during the hectic rush of the major incident.

'So what are you saying?'

'I'm saying that after the surgery I will be taking you away somewhere so you can rest and you and our baby will be taken care of. I know you love your job—God knows I understand that better than most—but you will not rush back to it and risk yourself or our baby.'

'Taking me where?'

'It will depend how your recovery goes. But if it's smooth then I have a place in Italy. I intend to take you there.'

'Italy?' she echoed weakly.

'It's quiet, and safe, and you can rest there without the worries of everyday life. I will ensure that you have dedicated specialists on hand, and your health and that of our baby will be of paramount importance.'

Vaguely she thought she ought to be objecting. Instead all she could ask was, 'Will you be there, too?'

'I have no intention of being anywhere else,' he gritted out.

Something a little too close to relief trickled through her, but she did her best to conceal it. There was no need for him to find out how dependent upon him she was starting to feel. He was spooked enough at the idea of emotional intimacy with her.

'Okay.'

'And we *will* marry, Saskia. For the baby's sake. I can assure you of that.'

The worst of it was that she had to bite her tongue not to simply agree to that, too. Even if he *was* doing it for the wrong reasons, part of her couldn't help but feel it was the right solution.

At least she would have him in her life. And after the last few days she was beginning to find it harder and harder to envisage a future with her baby and without Malachi closely entwined in it.

'We'll see,' she managed instead, acutely aware that this time it wasn't an outright refusal.

His eyes held hers and, try as she might, she couldn't seem to drag her gaze away. The stayed like that for longer than she could tell—an eternity, perhaps—until they heard the consultant returning and he finally dropped his hands.

She felt the loss acutely.

CHAPTER TEN

THE HELICOPTER TOUCHED down in the grounds of a fourteenth-century *castello*, complete with square tower, just as fresh flakes of snow were falling on the Tuscan mountains, which rose majestically around them. It was as though Malachi himself had commanded it.

The surgery a week ago had been a success, and the baby—a baby girl—appeared to be thriving. The fact that, although she had lost some amniotic fluid during the surgery, the levels had risen again very quickly post-surgery made Saskia feel as though her body was at least now doing what it was supposed to do. Although she hadn't voiced that particular dark thought to anyone—not even Malachi.

The strands which had been entangling the baby had all been cut, and already the swelling in the left foot had begun to reduce—although she would need Z-plasty for the grooves post-natally. The slight clubbing would also be corrected post-birth, with a brace, but to all intents and purposes she now seemed to be healthy and developing well.

And through it all Malachi had barely left her side. He'd made her feel cared for. Supported. It was little wonder that she felt more of a bond with him than ever, even if she knew it was hopeless and not a little foolhardy.

It was why now, as they descended the stairs from the helicopter, Saskia concentrated on taking in the breathtaking views.

If she hadn't been pregnant she would have been thrilled to be coming here and taking advantage of the skiing on offer, from the lava domes of Amiata to the ski slopes of Abetone. She knew from the few photos she'd seen around Malachi's apartment that he went glacial abseiling and scaling frozen waterfalls in his rare downtime. Now she realised that it must be here that he came to get away from it all.

What did it mean that he'd invited her into this private bolthole of his? Or was she reading too much into it?

She was still mulling it over as Malachi steered her around the helicopter and she finally turned towards the castle itself. It had taken a slow drive to the airfield, his private jet to Italy, and a helicopter ride to get here, but now that she had finally arrived she knew it was worth it.

It stole the very air from her lungs.

tionship with families like Izzy and Michelle he knew he was more than just financially invested. But Malachi, like his brother, Sol, was such a closed book that those few details were the sum of her knowledge.

It was all Saskia could do not to fall on this new scrap of information as if it was an oasis in the desert and she was a dying woman. But inside she was aching to know more. To understand what made Malachi who he was. To learn what drove him on.

Clearly he didn't intend to elaborate, and she tried not to feel hurt that, even after everything they'd been through with their own little miracle, he still didn't trust her enough to want to open up to her.

It ought to be the wake-up call she needed to remember to keep her guard up where Malachi Gunn was concerned. It was futile to keep wanting—imagining—more with him. In his eyes, their agreement was nothing more than the extension of a business agreement.

She forced herself to take a mouthful of the delicious biscuit. Then another. Anything but give in to the temptation to ask him more about himself and risk him shutting down on her.

But eventually the silence got to her. 'How long are you going to stay?' Saskia spoke at last, when they were alone again.

Really, after Imelda's comments about *the*

The place was magnificent. Stone walls with battlements, sloping bases and arched windows made it impossible for her not to imagine the frescoed walls and coffered ceilings which must surely lie inside. And the building's beauty was matched only by the oaks and cypresses and ilex shrubs which framed it.

'It's a wonder you ever come back to London,' she murmured to him, wondering why it felt so instantly comfortable, familiar to her.

Like a *home*.

It was almost a relief that her words were whipped away, unheard, by the roar of the heli.

Together they made their way across the lawns, glistening white under a thin veil of snow, to the housekeeper, who was waiting at the door.

'I told you to stay inside in the warmth, Imelda,' Malachi admonished, and Saskia was shocked to see the little, rotund older lady, with a faint West Country accent, throwing her arms around him and kissing him soundly on each cheek.

'I stayed at the door, didn't I?' she teased. 'It's so good to have you back, Malachi.' Then she turned with a warm smile. 'You must be Saskia—welcome to the *castello*. We're all just so delighted to meet the future Mrs Gunn.'

Saskia froze, but the woman seemed too caught up in the moment to notice.

'For pity's sake, bring the girl inside—she'll be catching her death. Shall I have hot drinks brought to you? The fires have been lit throughout.'

'Lovely, Imelda, thank you,' Malachi agreed. 'We shall be in the library, I think.'

'You have an English housekeeper?'

'I've known Imelda for almost fifteen years now. I bought this place with my first million, and her late husband was the builder who oversaw much of the renovation work.'

'You didn't do it yourself, then?' she teased.

'I did what I could.' Malachi shrugged. 'But I was still working a lot in the UK back then.'

She waited for him to elaborate further, but he didn't, instead ushering her through long criss-crossing corridors until they stepped through a door into what was clearly the library.

Old leather-bound tomes upon old leather-bound tomes lay behind pretty wrought-iron-framed doors. Wall-to-wall and floor-to-ceiling, save for the gargantuan stone fireplace with its timber mantelshelf which took up a third of one wall, and the two leaded windows, complete with deep sides and cushioned window seats, which nestled into the other.

As they stood in silence, the only noise was the welcoming crackle of the fire as the shadows began to dance around the room. It was only too

easy for Saskia to imagine whiling aw of her pregnancy here.

He ushered her into the room, tak tender care of her, before crossing the throw himself into a generous wingbac whilst she weighed up the merits of the the seating.

The window seats would afford her a view, but the wingback chair that matched M chi's was closer to that inviting fire. So she m her way over and there they sat, in compani able silence, until Imelda brought their drin along with some homemade biscuits, still war from the oven. The older woman fussed over he ensuring she was comfortable and pain-free, all the while bossing Malachi about and making certain that he was taking care of Saskia.

'She treats you more like a son than an employer,' Saskia said, smiling, when Imelda left the room at last, finally satisfied that her new patient was as comfortable as she could possibly be.

'In many ways she's the mother I never had,' Malachi answered—then stopped sharply, as though he hadn't intended to say anything at all.

'She obviously cares about you a great deal,' she ventured, then waited, hoping that he would say more.

Her heart flip-flopped madly. She knew he had set up the Care to Play charity because she'd met him at the ball, and judging by his close re-

future Mrs Gunn, there was only one question Saskia wanted to ask, but she feared it would start an argument and she didn't want that. Not when they'd only just arrived.

'I'm here to make sure you and the baby recuperate.'

Not exactly the answer she had been looking for.

'What about work?' she tried instead. 'How will you keep up to date?'

'What makes you think I'll be working?'

'Because you're a workaholic. You'll go crazy being here for too long and not overseeing your business.'

His lips pulled into a crooked smile, as if he was conceding her point. 'I can email…do video conferences.'

'It's beautiful here. I can see why you would enjoy bringing lots of people to see it.'

'Are you fishing, Saskia?' he asked mildly. 'Because I can tell you it isn't one of your more attractive qualities.'

Had she been fishing? She hadn't intended to, but she supposed it was a possibility. Was she here because she was the mother of his baby— someone special—or did he bring many of his 'dates'—for want of a better term—to his private *castello*?

She discreetly released her grip on the arms of her chair, but it was too much to hope Malachi wouldn't notice. His sharp eyes missed nothing. But she was surprised when he answered.

'I don't make it a habit of bringing people here, no. In fact, you are the only person, other than Sol, I have ever brought here. But you shouldn't read too much into that.'

Her heart jolted. She fought to remain passive. To remind herself that it wasn't really about her at all.

'Because I'm pregnant with your child?' she asserted quietly.

He didn't reply but he did incline his head, if only a fraction. She told herself she wasn't disappointed.

'Is that why you brought me here, Malachi? Because of the baby and so that I could rest? Or to further the notion that you had back in the UK that I would marry you?'

He eyed her neutrally, giving nothing away. It caused a thread of irritation to weave its way through her.

'It seems daft to pretend it isn't part of your plan,' she asserted, 'since it was practically the first thing Imelda mentioned when I stepped off that helicopter.'

'I am not *pretending* anything,' he replied, his voice calm. 'I simply don't believe this is the best time to be discussing matters which so…unsettled you last time, Saskia. As you just said yourself, you're supposed to be resting. Stress-free.'

'You've whisked me thousands of miles away, first by private plane and then by helicopter...' She cocked her head to one side. 'And now I'm sitting in a beautiful room, in front of a glorious fire, replete. I hardly think it's the most agitating of circumstances. When do you expect this marriage of ours to take place?'

He looked momentarily irritated, but then smoothed it away quickly. Oddly, the fact that he could master his emotions so easily only peeved her all the more.

'When, Malachi?'

He met her gaze, his eyebrows cocked slightly, as though she was a half-irritating, half-amusing nuisance.

'We will be married by the end of the week.'

Not a suggestion or a possibility, but a statement.

Saskia shuffled in her chair, incensed. 'Is that what you think?'

'You're getting worked up,' he said calmly.

'Do you wonder?' she seethed. 'So, tell me this—what is this *marriage* idea of yours going to look like? How do you suppose it will work?'

'I think this conversation is best left for another day.'

'I don't,' she objected. 'I mean, are you suggesting staying married until the baby is born, or staying married beyond that? If so, then how long? Is it to be a marriage in name only, or are you still suggesting we enjoy certain…shall we say…*benefits*?'

'So many questions…' He clicked his tongue softly. 'Yet you didn't think to ask a single one of them before boarding my plane. Almost as if a part of you wanted to come with me regardless.'

She wrinkled her nose, hating the way he seemed to be able to read into her mind and see her own questions which lay there, jumbled within.

If she'd sought to shame him, she realised she'd misjudged him. He didn't bristle, or take the bait. He merely stretched out his legs all the more, giving the illusion that he didn't have a care in the world.

She felt like launching something at him, but she only had a soft cushion. And, anyway, what good would that do?

'You are not the only one who has spent every waking moment worrying about our baby, *zvyozdochka*.'

His tone was like velvet, but she heard the hard steel beneath it.

'But that isn't what this is about, is it? The simple truth is that you don't find the idea of marriage to me as objectionable as you'd like to make out. Or maybe it's more that you no longer find it objectionable after what you've been through the past week. Tell me why that is.'

Could he hear the sound of her blood rushing

around her body? Because to her it was practically deafening. She couldn't tell him that it was because she feared she was falling for him. That his care and loyalty these past few weeks had made her feel more secure than Andy had done in all their years together.

'I never actually said I found it objectionable,' she prevaricated.

'I believe your precise words were "passion is overrated". You were very certain that it shouldn't be a business proposition, and then you proceeded to assert that, "We had a one-night stand. It's over." And that you didn't even want me "like that" any more.'

'Have you got a photographic memory or something?' she demanded sarcastically, in an effort to hide how shaken she felt.

She didn't really expect him to respond. But it seemed that Malachi revelled in catching her off guard.

'Eidetic, if we're being accurate.' He folded his arms across his chest. A move which only served to emphasis the broadness of his shoulders. 'But that's by the by. I'm more interested in how, moments after that bold little statement of yours, you ended up half-naked on my bed whilst I used my mouth to make you scream. I'm sure you remember?'

Oh, yes, she remembered, all right. All too gloriously vividly. Indeed, it was galling how her mouth threatened to dry up just at the mere memory.

She sent silent thanks for the fact that she was post-op. She might not have had the will to resist him if they'd been standing here under different circumstances.

'We slept together. Again.' She lifted her shoulders. 'But I still don't know what your intentions are for any marriage between us.'

'My *intentions*?' He barked out a sound which might have been a laugh, but she knew wasn't. 'You make it sound so old-fashioned and formal. Like you're still waiting for some romantic declaration of love and commitment which I can't give you. An echo of that profound passion your parents had.'

'And you still scoff at me for that,' she bristled, heat creeping into her tone as she tried to quash the sense of unease which was creeping up on her.

Malachi couldn't know the truth about her parents. She didn't want his sympathy or his pity. She couldn't bear it.

'But just because you never experienced parents who loved one another it doesn't mean you can disparage others who have. And just because you don't believe in it, it doesn't mean it can't exist.'

'You don't know what you're talking about.' His face hardened instantly.

With a thrill, Saskia realised she had some-how got under his skin. She didn't know how, but if this was her one chance then she wasn't about to back down.

She softened her tone until it was almost breezily dismissive. 'I think I know enough.'

'You're wrong.'

'What is there to know?' She made herself shrug. 'You're a tortured man, damaged by his past and a childhood in which he was never loved. It's all terribly clichéd. And now you keep yourself emotionally unavailable and you mock those who might want something more from a relationship.'

'You're walking a very thin line, *zvyozdochka*,' warned Malachi. 'You don't have a clue what you're talking about.'

'Maybe. Maybe not. But whose fault is that?'

'So you think by provoking me I'll tell you what you want to know about me?'

'I think you'll either tell me or you won't. Whether I support you or provoke you won't change anything. I simply decided I didn't want to sit back and let you disparage *my* memories just because you don't understand them.'

'You misunderstand.' His eyes bored into her, practically pinning her to the seat. 'I understand exactly what your memories are. I just don't agree with the way you interpret them.'

'Sorry?'

'You're holding on to this great love affair between your parents and you're searching for the same thing. But you'll never find it because you aren't as selfish and as cruel as they were.'

'My parents were *not* selfish and cruel,' she denied vehemently, because if she was forceful enough then maybe she could make it true. 'They loved each other fiercely.'

'And what about you?' he pushed.

'Of course they loved me.'

He was pushing her dangerously close to the edge, and she felt as though she was clinging on with the tops of her fingers. But she couldn't let him know that. She wouldn't let him see.

'They adored me!' she cried, emotion threatening to clog her throat.

Malachi opened his mouth. Then closed it. His face was shuttered again, and a fresh wave of frustration powered through her.

'So that's it?' she challenged. 'You push so far and then you back away when things start to get hot?'

'I don't think this is a conversation that will get us anywhere,' he replied smoothly. 'Especially not when you're supposed to be recuperating. So, if you've quite finished making up objections, I suggest I show you to your suite, so you can clean up after the flight and rest, even sleep if you wish.'

He stretched out his long, muscular legs and

stood with all the grace and power of some glossy big cat in its natural habitat. And equally as lethal.

When he reached out to offer her his hand she briefly considered refusing his help and getting to her feet by herself. But the truth was that between the flight, the operation, and the baby scare, she was feeling far more drained than she'd realised.

Still, she plastered on a bright smile. 'I'm fine.'

Malachi looked unimpressed. 'Your doctor may not have put you on bed rest, but if you don't do what she said in terms of taking it easy, don't think I won't put you in bed myself.'

Saskia swallowed, trying not to focus on the X-rated images which had instantly slipped into her brain at his words, or on the memories of what had happened between them every other time they'd been in the vicinity of a bed.

Malachi had paused, too, as though he was fighting a similar battle.

She followed him through the house, back to the imposing hallway, up the wide, sweeping staircase and along the first-floor corridor, in silence.

Nevertheless, she was sure she didn't imagine that his voice was fractionally hoarser when he spoke again.

'This is your suite.' He stopped outside a set

of heavy walnut double doors. 'Dinner will be ready at seven. I'll wait for you in the hallway.'

Saskia was torn between the elegant formality and the fear that it made things too clinical—too detached—between them.

'I'm not entirely sure I'll have anything appropriate to wear. I only brought a small case.' She cast him a vaguely accusatory glare. 'You didn't exactly give me much of a chance to pack.'

'I seriously doubt you had much to choose from, anyway,' he eyed her shrewdly. 'Or do you already have a full maternity wardrobe?'

Her hand flew to her rounded belly on cue. He had a point.

'Fortunately,' he continued easily, 'I had the foresight to have some clothes delivered once I decided we would be coming here. Imelda had them put away in your suite.'

'I don't know whether to feel flattered or insulted.' Her voice was clipped.

'I suggest you just accept it for what it is,' suggested Malachi. 'Rather than overthinking everything you come across.'

Before she could answer he turned away and sauntered up the corridor, hands in pockets. Possibly to his own suite, which was no doubt located as far away from hers as it was possible to get, she decided.

Which was just fine.

CHAPTER ELEVEN

SASKIA STARED AROUND her suite, slightly agog. It had been decades since she'd been part of Hollywood royalty, but she still recalled the beauty of the places she'd lived and the hotels in which she'd stayed.

Malachi's *castello* beat every one of those hands-down.

The first room she'd entered was, she realised after rather a long moment, a living space. Her own private living space. The suite was already generous, but the high ceilings, with their ornate friezes, made it feel positively expansive. Carved wooden shutters framed huge leaded glass windows, and two oversized plush couches sat delicately in the space.

Saskia crossed the room to the next set of double doors, opening them almost tentatively. Another high-ceilinged ornate space lay beyond, only in the middle of this one sat an enormous four-poster bed—arguably as big as her entire bedroom back in her apartment. Underfloor heating discreetly warmed the space, whilst the stunning parquet made her itch to walk across it in her bare feet.

If it hadn't been for her post-op state she might even have twirled around the room like a ballerina. It was such a beautiful, magical space.

She opened a door on what presumably had to be the bathroom, only to find it was a walk-in closet about the size of her kitchen, full of carelessly beautiful clothes that her fingers ached to touch.

Then, finally, she found it. The bathroom. A glorious limestone affair with practically a spa-sized tub for a bath and a waterfall for a shower.

It was enough to make Saskia wish she never had to leave.

Except, she reminded herself fiercely, *for the fact that it belongs to Malachi.*

Wandering in, she found some pins to put her hair up, let her clothes lie where they dropped, and allowed the shower to call to her. It was a revival such as she had never had before. Not just sluicing away the drudge of the journey, but also the crud of the last few weeks.

She washed it all down the long-grid gutter as though it had never existed. Including the last conversation with Malachi, which had seemed to go completely the wrong way. Like a giant step back after all the shuffling forward they had managed together this past week.

It wasn't how she'd wanted it to go. She certainly hadn't wanted to argue…

Saskia had no idea how long she stood there, letting the water pound down over her body, and letting her mind clear of some of its recent obstacles. She only knew that by the time she emerged she felt lighter, happier than she had in a while.

She padded softly through to the bedroom, climbed up onto the high bed and sank back into the downy pillows, intending to stay there for only a few minutes.

She fell into a deep, dreamless sleep within seconds.

It might have helped if she hadn't looked quite so devastating, Malachi thought several hours later, as Saskia walked down the stairs in a figure-hugging maternity dress which showed off the growing bump—*his baby*—perfectly. It also made something thicken and tighten within him.

But, more importantly, she looked well. As though she was recovering more from the operation with every single hour that passed.

It was odd how terrified he'd been this past week. Strange how he hadn't noticed this…this *emotion* which had been building up inside him ever since Saskia had told him that she was pregnant until he'd had to face the fear that she could be about to lose the baby.

That had been the moment he'd realised that

he was attached. That he wanted the child—and Saskia—in his life.

Selfish, maybe, since he could never be the kind of man, or husband, she clearly wanted. And this afternoon's conversation should have been a warning. The thing to make him reconsider this ludicrous idea of marriage.

There was no avoiding the fact that Saskia wanted the impossible. She wanted a magical love affair, to be madly in love—and that was the one thing he couldn't offer her.

He didn't even believe in it.

He'd spent the past few hours stalking the *castello* in a grim mood. He had never intended the argument between them to get so heated. He shouldn't have let her get under his skin the way she had. But that was what Saskia had been doing ever since their first encounter at the charity ball all those months ago.

Feisty, and funny, and sexy. He'd been hooked from the start.

Even if he hadn't overheard her telling that silly nurse that she was pregnant, he would have found an excuse to slip back into her life. *Him*. The man who was famous for never getting too close to anyone.

Now he would be tied to Saskia, and the baby she was carrying, for the rest of their lives—and it didn't fill him with horror in any way, even though he knew it should.

But that still didn't mean he was able to spout all the poetry and words of love that she seemed to have decided went hand-in-glove with marriage.

He couldn't make those grand romantic gestures which meant nothing unless you treated the other person with consideration and respect every single day.

No, he couldn't give her the fancy words, but he could offer her loyalty. Commitment. Honour. He would care for their child, and for her, for the rest of his life. He knew from experience that that was far more precious than an intense, passionate fire which would eventually fade and die.

It was only a shame that Saskia didn't see it the same way. Yet. But Malachi was confident that, in time, she would come to appreciate the value in it.

'You look beautiful,' he murmured, holding out his arm as she reached the bottom few steps, and he wondered if he'd ever be able to let go.

Her head snapped up. She eyed him suspiciously, as if looking for a trap, but he simply led her to the dining room, where the table was laid out just for them.

It was time.

It was only when Saskia saw the ring box that she realised this dinner was a proposal. Malachi was going to ask her the question she'd spent months telling herself she *didn't* dream of him asking.

Dimly, she was aware that he was saying the words, but it was as though she was on her own operating table, succumbing to the effects of an anaesthetic: aware of what was going on, but not really present in it any longer.

He was asking her to marry him. And, although almost every fibre of her hungered to say *yes*, the logical part of her brain knew she had to demur.

What choice did she really have?

Her body actually shook with the effort of holding itself together. Like the harmonic tremors you felt in the ground before a volcano erupted. Only Saskia wasn't about to flare up. Instead she was terrified of breaking down. Especially in front of Malachi.

When he finally finished speaking she forced herself to look up from the ring and into his gaze, and suddenly it was all worse.

So much worse.

She tried to suck a breath into her constricted chest. She'd been here once before, when she'd been ready to accept his proposal—such as it was—only for him to turn around and rescind it.

And it had hurt far more than it had had any right to.

More than her parents' betrayal. More than Andy's betrayal.

Her feeling of rejection had terrified her. Because if he could hurt her that much in a matter of months, what would it be like to marry the man and submit to the illusion that they were more than just co-parents to a baby conceived on a one-night stand?

So Saskia opened her mouth and uttered the only objection she could think of, under the circumstances.

'Why?'

He blinked.

'Why?' he echoed, and the hint of disbelief was almost her undoing.

'Why do you want to marry me, Malachi?'

And she was ashamed that it was less a stalling tactic and more a plea. As if a part of her really believed he would say the words she needed to hear.

'Give me a real reason.'

For a moment he seemed at a loss for words. And then he regrouped.

'This conversation again, *zvyozdochka*?' He managed to inject as much of a yawn into his voice as possible without actually yawning. 'It is becoming boring.'

'Maybe for you,' she shot back, determined to appear undaunted. 'But since I haven't had a straight answer out of you yet, I can't agree.'

'You're the mother of my unborn baby, Saskia.'

His voice was low and even, if a little surprised. 'How much more "real" a reason do you need?'

She didn't know if it was the words or the easy control in Malachi's voice which cut through her most sharply. Surely if he felt anything towards her whatsoever there would be at least a hint of emotion in his words?

'I want...*more*,' she whispered at length.

'More?'

His gaze darkened, his forehead knitting together. She could almost feel the coldness beginning to roll off him.

'Like meaningless declarations of love, perhaps?'

'Why do they have to be meaningless?' Saskia asked, not sure whether she meant it as a plea or an accusation.

'Because they're just words,' he growled. 'They bring nothing to the table.'

'They do for me.'

Before she realised what she was doing she was moving her hand across the table. Stopping it halfway between the two of them. He stared at it for a moment, as if actually trying to work out what she was doing. But he didn't reach his own hand out. Instead he placed his fingers together and dropped his hands to his lap.

'Not if they came from me.'

He shook his head, and the words were so

harsh, so threaded with pain, that it almost broke Saskia apart.

'I doubt I even have the capacity for love.'

'I think you do.'

Again he shook his head, and when he spoke, his voice was so raw and rough she was sure she could feel it actually abrading her.

'No. And even if I did it would be so fractured, so tainted, that it would do more harm to the recipient than anything else.'

'No…'

There had to be more. They hadn't spent the past few weeks getting closer just for nothing. Surely?

'Love from someone like me wouldn't be a gift, *zvyozdochka*. It would be a curse.'

'You make it sound like you're a victim of your past, but the truth is that you're a liar.'

She had no idea where the strength had come from, but Saskia seized it with both hands and let it drag her along. Because it was easier to bear than the pain.

'I'd prefer it if you didn't complicate things further by proposing marriage when all I am to you is a complication.'

'We aren't a couple. We had a one-night stand—uncharacteristic for both of us, but there you have it—and now you're carrying my child. What else would you call it, *zvyozdochka*?'

Saskia opened her mouth to reply, but the

words didn't come. Or at least the words that did come sounded distasteful on her tongue, and she couldn't bring herself to utter them.

Malachi had a point. Their baby wasn't planned, and the circumstances weren't enviable, which made it a complication. The difference was that, to her, it was an unexpectedly joyous complication, whilst to Malachi it was apparently on a par with the irritations he experienced in business every day.

His solution was typically practical and logical. But it wasn't emotional. And that was what she wanted it to be more than anything else.

Without warning, all the air seemed to whoosh out of her. It was all she could do to hold her head up and not deflate right there in front of Malachi.

'We had passion,' she whispered.

His face hardened, the angular lines of his jaw suddenly becoming harsher. Almost cutting.

'That was about sex. Not love.'

'How do you know it isn't both?' She knew she was clutching at hope but she couldn't stop herself. 'If you won't ever give love a chance?'

'I don't believe in it. It's an illusion,' he refuted fiercely. 'Passion comes with a price, and it's always one that's too high. I won't do that to you, *or* our child.'

'Malachi—'

'I told you that from the start,' he cut in, refusing to listen to her.

It was like a howl inside her. Long and low, tugging at her very soul. She'd laid it out there—laid herself out there—and he didn't want her. He never had.

'You're right.' How her voice managed to sound so calm, so neutral, was a small miracle. 'You told me from the start that you couldn't offer me more than your duty. Your responsibility. But I thought there was more to us than that. Or at least I wanted to believe that there was.'

'Because you're carrying around some non-existent romantic notion based on what you want to remember about what your parents had. You compare everything to that. And there's no way anything you find will ever match up. It's impossible.'

'This is what you were saying this afternoon,' she ground out. 'Telling me that my parents didn't care enough when I *remember* how much they loved me.'

'But not enough for them to stick around.'

'They were in a car crash. They couldn't help that.'

'*Zvyozdochka*, they were arguing. I looked into it after that night in my apartment, when you refused to see sense and just marry me. They were having another of their infamous fights which blazed almost as brightly as their so-called great love. They were drunk, and fighting, and people had heard them threatening to harm each other. And then your father apparently ran into a tree on a straight, well-lit stretch of road, with no other cars in sight. Your mother, supposedly unable to bear the pain of his death, took an accidental overdose.'

'*Accidental!*' she cried, anguished. 'You just said it yourself. They were both *accidents*.'

'No, *zvyozdochka*, they were covered up and sold to the grieving public as accidents. But I think we both know the truth.'

'You're wrong!' She shook her head, but the shaking that had started from her toes and was working its way up her body told her differently.

'I don't think so,' he said quietly. She might have thought even sadly. 'You know exactly what happened and so do I. Yet you've put them on a pedestal and sold it to yourself as some grand love affair, when the truth is that you're using it as some impossible standard you know you can never achieve because it's a way for you to stay emotionally out of reach.'

'That's insane,' she muttered.

Only she had a feeling it made awful, terrible sense. How had she never realised this before? Or had she, on some level?

'You say you want what they had, but you don't, *zvyozdochka*. You're not capable of it because you aren't as selfish as them. You could never do to your child what they did to you. You could never leave our daughter.'

'That makes no sense…' whispered Saskia.

'It does—and you know it does.'

She didn't want to answer. She didn't want to engage with him. But she couldn't help herself.

'I think you're attacking me because it's easier than looking at yourself,' she challenged, not caring that her breathing was shallow and fast, or that she sounded as though she'd run a marathon. 'You're pretending you don't feel something I know you feel.'

'You're mistaken.'

'You and I had an arrangement that was all about practicality. We didn't need to…to sleep together, but we did. Because we *wanted* to. You might tell yourself that you aren't capable of love, but you are.'

He glared at her for a long moment, and Saskia realised she couldn't even breathe.

Until, at last, he spoke. 'Then perhaps I'm just not capable of loving *you*.'

Rejection lodged in her throat, thick and bitter-tasting. Saskia struggled to swallow it down.

'Perhaps not,' she rasped out. 'But I don't think it's that. And I don't think you do, either.'

'All I can offer you is everything I've already promised. I will be the best father anyone could possibly be to this child. And I will be the best provider. I will take of my family the way I have always done. You'll want for nothing—I can promise you that. But I can't promise you love, or happy-ever-afters. I can't pretend this is some great love story. I am who I am, Saskia.'

'You're so much more than you think,' Saskia whispered. 'But if I can't make you see that then perhaps I'm wrong for you.'

'Perhaps you are,' he gritted out, thrusting his chair back abruptly and standing. 'But I will not see our child suffer for our mistakes. We will marry, and we will provide a united front for this child.'

Malachi had no idea what had just happened. Or, more to the point, what he had just allowed to happen.

His head told him that he had done the right thing, but his chest was tight and angry. Full of a churning sense of remorse. Both for what he'd said and the way he'd spoken to her.

But it was for the best, he told himself furiously.

Everything he'd said was the truth. He couldn't be the man she wanted him to be—the kind of man who professed love—he could only be who he was and hope that was enough.

Evidently it wasn't enough for Saskia.

She wanted the words. The flowers. The poetry. All the things he couldn't—*wouldn't?*—give her.

He stalked the grounds of his *castello*, glaring into the darkness to see if perhaps the night sky had fallen in. After all, what other reason could there be for what was going on here?

His head was constantly full of thoughts of Saskia. And it wasn't helped by the idea of her soft, wet body against him, on him, around him. Even at work the meatiest of contracts hadn't been able to distract him from her.

He scowled at the sky even harder—but, no, it was most certainly up where it should be. What was more, it positively twinkled with the prettiest stars, free of urban light pollution, almost as if it were entertained by his uncharacteristic reverie.

It was galling.

He could take off for a night run, go a few rounds in the *castello*'s well-appointed gym, or swim lap after lap until his body ached. But he suspected it would do little to numb his brain from the effect Saskia was having on him.

How was it that she could make him feel powerful and powerless all at the same time?

This wasn't him. This wasn't the untouchable man he'd turned himself into once he'd finally dragged himself and Sol from the bowels of a childhood caring for their junkie mother.

He'd sworn to himself all those years ago that he would never let another person get under his skin like that. Aside from his brother, he'd vowed he would never permit anyone to venture this far into his life. A wife, a family, children. It was never going to be for him. He'd never wanted it.

Yet here Saskia was. Pregnant.

He had no name for this heavy, full feeling which was building in his chest with every passing day, but it didn't seem to be regret. Or resentment.

In someone else he might have thought it was... *joy*. Or happiness. Or even love. But this wasn't someone else—this was him. And he didn't feel those things. He never had. The closest he'd ever come to feeling love was for his kid brother, but it wasn't the kind of unfettered, wholehearted emotion that normal people seemed to feel.

He wouldn't know how to feel that way if he tried.

With a growl of frustration Malachi spun away from the lake, in which he could suddenly see his own reflection all too clearly, bright in the moonlight. He didn't think he liked what he saw—and stalked back to his room.

He was hauling off his constricting shirt even as he pushed through the door to his suite. Minutes later he was beating a punching bag in the corner of the gym as though he could mete out punishment for his every last frustration and knock his self-doubt into submission. Banish the emotions he hadn't felt since he was an eight-year-old boy, running errands for the local gang just to get enough money to put coins in the electricity meter and a scant bit of food on the table for five-year-old Sol.

He had no idea how long he stayed in the gym. After the boxing he took a long run on the treadmill, imagining in his head that he was actually running through the vineyards outside, which lay all around this stunning valley. Finally he dived into the still waters of the indoor pool and swam one hundred exhausting lengths, then a hundred more, and then another for good measure.

When he finally—*finally*—allowed himself to stop, to breathe, to look up, it was to see Saskia curled up on the window seat of the suite he had given her, a book in her hand.

But she wasn't reading. She was watching him.

He could feel it.

Her eyes caressed his skin as surely as if it had been her hands themselves. How he wished that were the case. He wanted her. He *hungered* for her.

And he did not hunger. Ever.

Yet now it rolled through him like the thunder for which this valley was so well known at this time of year. Raw and uncontrollable.

It was all Malachi could do to keep himself in the water. To turn his back on the woman who affected him in such a primal way. To spin his body in the pool and cut through the water for another hundred lengths.

Because if he hadn't he feared he would have hauled his body out and gone to find her.

CHAPTER TWELVE

'WHAT IS THE matter with you, *bratik*?' Malachi glared balefully across his office to where Sol was helping himself to Malachi's freshly ground coffee and pastries, as he did every time he ventured across town to MIG International's offices.

Malachi told himself he'd returned to the UK because he was needed at work. He knew the truth wasn't anything like that. Still, he comforted himself with the assurance that he'd left Saskia in good hands, with the team of medical experts in Italy.

It wasn't helping him to concentrate.

'What?' Sol cocked an eyebrow, before striding over to flop in a comfortable chair.

'You're full of the joys of spring,' he grumbled.

'And *you're* grouchy and on edge.' Sol eyed him shrewdly. 'More so than usual, that is. Though I wouldn't have thought that was possible.'

'Funny.'

'Thanks.'

'Idiot.' Sol shrugged, inhaling a couple of pastries, whole.

It wasn't that he wasn't happy to see his brother, Malachi decided, it was more that right now he would have preferred to be alone, to throw himself into the work he'd missed whilst he'd been in Italy with Saskia.

Or alone to stew, a cynical voice needled.

The past week had been hell. Like some kind of torture he hadn't known existed. He saw Saskia everywhere he went. He could hear her voice, gently teasing him about all the things he did. Like some kind of haunting such as he had never believed in.

But then, he hadn't believed in a lot of things before Saskia had come along.

This intense, yearning sensation which barrelled around his chest, for one thing. Guilt, probably. Remorse. What else would have been mushrooming inside him for so long now?

He didn't know and he didn't care.

He was so lost in his own thoughts that he answered his brother's next question on autopilot, not really paying attention to what was said until Sol's next statement jarred him.

'You and I have always said that we aren't built for commitment or love...' his brother began slowly. 'That everything *she* put us through destroyed that in us. But what if we're wrong, Mal?

What if you and I have *always* been capable of love?'

'This discussion is over,' Malachi ground out.

It was as if his brother was echoing everything that had been going on in Italy, and right now it was the last conversation Malachi wanted to have with anyone. But still he didn't move.

Did his brother know about Saskia?

Did the entire hospital?

Sol shifted, looking oddly uncomfortable.

'There's always been love between you and me,' he said, as though he was repeating someone else's words and wasn't quite sure if he was doing it correctly. 'It may be a different kind of love, but it's love nonetheless.'

'Where did *those* pearls of wisdom come from?' Malachi tried to snort—but, inexplicably, he lacked the scorn that would normally have come so easily.

Sol paused, seeming to consider what to say. 'I don't know,' he concluded at last.

And, despite his own worries, Malachi couldn't help worrying about his kid brother, the way he always had as the big brother. Hadn't he been mentioning Saskia's flatmate a lot recently…?

'A woman?'

'No…' denied Sol unconvincingly. Then, 'Maybe…'

'Anouk?'

'Are you going to take the proverbial?' He glowered at Malachi, clearly expecting the usual ribbing. But for once Malachi didn't feel like it.

'Maybe another time.'

Sol narrowed his eyes thoughtfully and Malachi pretended to ignore him.

'Yeah, then,' Sol admitted. 'Anouk.'

It was enough to finally get his attention. If Sol, the perennial playboy, could be falling for a woman, it had to say something.

'Something's going on between you?'

'I don't know. Maybe.'

Malachi knew he should back away, but he couldn't. It was too coincidental.

'Serious?'

Sol hesitated. 'Maybe. She's the reason I came here today, at least.'

His brother studied him, cool and perceptive. 'What do you need?' Malachi asked at length.

'You have people who can track stuff down for you, right?'

Malachi inclined his head.

'I want you to track down all you can on this man.' Sol flicked though his phone and found the notepad before spinning it across the desk to him. 'He died thirteen years ago, but he used to live there.'

Wordlessly Malachi read the screen and made a note of the information. He didn't even question it. If Sol needed it that was his business. Besides, if he kept his nose out of his brother's life maybe Sol would return the favour.

'Do you think you can do this without hurting her, Sol?' Malachi heard himself saying the words.

'Sorry?'

'Settling down with Anouk. Do you think you can do that?'

He knew it came across as a challenge, but he hadn't intended it to. All he wanted was to understand. To be sure it wasn't just himself making a mistake.

'I'm not settling down,' Sol denied.

'Then why do you care? I mean, I get that you care about your patients, and the kids at the centre. But I've never known you to care about a woman enough to ask for my help.'

'She's…different.'

Malachi knew his brother was choosing his words carefully. Almost too carefully.

'But that doesn't mean there's anything serious between us.'

'Right…'

Malachi pushed his chair back abruptly and stood up, moving to the window to look out. Not at anything in particular—just as a way to escape the confines of the room, which suddenly felt a little stifling.

Not that it made any difference. Wherever

he looked Saskia was back, plaguing his every thought.

Still, it caught him out when Sol suddenly spoke.

'Who is she, Mal?'

Malachi swung around but said nothing. He had no idea what he *could* say. He didn't even know what he thought.

Still, he didn't like the way his brother was watching him a little too shrewdly. As if he knew what was going on.

'I think I prefer the Sol who just beds women and moves on,' Malachi bit out. 'You're acting like a lost puppy—Anouk's lost puppy, to be exact.'

'Sod off,' Sol said casually, before standing up and sauntering over to the sideboard for more pastries. 'I'm no one's puppy.'

'Not usually, no.' Malachi shrugged. 'You're usually fending them off with a stick.'

'What? Puppies?' Sol quipped.

'Puppies, women, little old ladies...' Malachi folded his arms over his chest and shrugged. 'But I've never seen you look at anyone the way I saw you look at that one the night of the gala.'

'Her name's Anouk,' Sol corrected instinctively, realising too late that he'd been baited.

Interesting, Malachi considered.

'And I didn't look at her in any particularly special way.'

Malachi said nothing.

'No clever quip?' Sol demanded, when he clearly couldn't stand the heavy silence any longer.

'I told you—not this time.'

He could hardly batter his kid brother about Anouk when he had left Saskia at his *castello*, four months pregnant, in Imelda's care.

What the hell was he even *doing* here in the UK?

'What's going on, Mal?' Sol asked suddenly.

'Nothing.'

'You're being cagey.'

'Not really,' Mal dismissed casually. Arguably a little too casually. 'No more so than you, anyway.'

'You're kidding, right?' Sol shook his head in disbelief.

'Not particularly.'

'Fine.' Leaning back on the sideboard, Sol eyed his brother. 'Time to tell me something I don't know, Mal. If you've got the balls for it.'

And just like that they were two kids again, and Sol was pressing him about where he'd been that first time he'd done a job for the Mullen brothers.

It was so random, and yet it felt so appropriate. And before he knew it Mal heard himself reply.

'I always thought a wife, a family, wasn't for us. Not after everything with *her*.'

Sol didn't answer, but Mal knew they both understood he was talking about their mother.

'I always thought I'd done that bit. I'd endured that responsibility. I never wanted to do it again.'

'But now...?' Sol prompted.

'Lately... I don't know.' Malachi swung around from the window almost angrily. 'Forget it. I'm just... Forget I said anything.'

In over two decades they hadn't talked about any of this. About feelings. The Gunn brothers had never bought into the caring/sharing thing. Now Malachi wondered if they'd been wrong to bottle things up.

'Are we capable of it, do you think, Mal?' asked Sol.

He frowned. 'Of what?'

'Of...love.'

It was so out of the blue that Mal couldn't even begin to order his thoughts.

'You *love* Anouk?'

Sol scoffed, but there was an expression in his eyes that had him convinced his brother wasn't just kidding around.

'Don't be stupid,' Sol said. 'I'm not saying that. It's just hypothetical.'

He didn't believe his brother—but that wasn't his main issue.

'Hypothetically, I don't even know if we have that capacity,' Malachi gritted out unexpectedly. 'But maybe the question should be, do we deserve it? More pertinently, does *any* woman deserve to be subjected to our love, *bratik*? Whatever that is.'

Sol stared at him blankly for an age.

'So…you and Saskia?'

'I don't wish to discuss it.' Malachi cut him off harshly.

And then Sol shocked him by placing his hands on Malachi's desk and addressing him urgently.

'But you need to. Right here, right now. Our mother ruined our childhood. It's time we both decided whether we're going to let her ruin our futures, too.'

Saskia knew he was back in Italy the moment she walked through the gym door the next morning. It was something in the air. The way the hairs on her arms lifted as if in anticipation.

She wondered when he'd returned from the UK. And why. The last few nights had been horrendous, tossing and turning and wondering if Malachi was even going to bother coming back.

Her stomach still churned with the idea that he might not. She'd have been trapped with no way out.

So why was it that she didn't feel remotely hemmed-in when Mal was around?

He was the one who had insisted on this sham marriage, on her moving into his apartment, on them forging some kind of relationship, if only for the sake of their unborn baby.

But you didn't have to agree, pointed out a calm, rational voice which sounded altogether too much like her best friend, Anouk.

Shoving it aside, Saskia threw open the door to the gym and marched boldly inside.

She stopped.

Swallowed.

Tried not to stare.

Knowing Malachi was in here all hours, running, swimming, keeping out of her way, had been one thing. The sight of him now, training with a Mu ren Zhuang—all graceful power, his body in complete control of each perfectly landed strike, his bare chest glistening with a sheen of sweat—was enough to steal the breath from her lungs.

He didn't appear to have spotted her, and she knew she should probably alert him to her presence, but all she could do was stand and watch. Mesmerised.

Time passed, but Saskia wasn't even aware of it. Only of the rhythmic, elegant pace of his movements. The hypnotic nature of his training.

And then he placed a plastic water bottle on the top of the training post, kicked the post with one leg to catapult the bottle into the air, then spun around and kicked it with the other foot.

It came thundering through the air towards

her, and before she could stop herself Saskia let out a surprised squeak and launched herself sideways.

Malachi was across the room in an instant. 'What are you doing in here?'

'Looking for you,' she retorted, tilting her chin up in defiance at his vaguely accusatory tone. 'You're back, then.'

'Evidence would support that observation,' he returned.

Any other woman might have balked at the dangerous edge to his voice. Saskia decided that she didn't care. Or, at least, what did she have to lose?

'I wouldn't have been surprised if you'd left me here. In the capable hands of Imelda, of course.'

For a moment she thought he wasn't going to answer. So she wasn't prepared when that dark, impenetrable expression eased and he nodded at her.

'Perhaps I was going to. But I thought better of it.'

For a split second she faltered, but then caught herself. If she didn't take advantage of this moment she would be a fool. Because he could shut her out at any moment and then where would she be?

Her heart thundered.

'Why?' she asked.

'You once asked me to tell you something

about myself. Something that wasn't carefully crafted by MIG International's PR machine.'

The roaring in her ears, which had started slowly the moment she'd walked into the gym, became almost deafening. He couldn't be opening up to her—that would be too much to hope for.

'You refused,' she managed instead.

'So now I'm telling you.'

He shrugged, but the dismissive gesture didn't fool her for a moment.

'My parents had a similar sort of ridiculous grand love affair to what your parents had. Passion and drama with a sprinkling of volatility, just like your parents—though it ended rather differently. The first few years of my life were fine. Better than fine. We didn't have much money, but we were a family.'

Her heart was already twisting painfully, folding in on itself even before he'd finished.

'And then my father died. He was a prize fighter, and one night he sustained a head injury. A bleed on the brain.'

'How old were you?' she asked, shocked.

'I was five and Sol was two.'

Her brain began to turn. 'Is that why your brother chose neurosurgery?'

'Maybe.' He lifted his shoulders again. 'Anyway, the same night my mother began her descent into drugs. It was slow at first, but it gathered momentum quickly. By the time I was eight I was caring for her and for my brother full-time.'

'You were a young carer?' she realised, wondering why she hadn't seen it before. How had she been so blind? 'That's why you set up Care to Play?'

And it was why he was insisting on taking responsibility for her and for their baby. It was in Malachi's make-up. It was who he was. The fact that it was *her* carrying his baby had no bearing on it whatsoever. She was nothing special to him. She never would be. She was just the woman who had fallen pregnant with his baby.

It was all finally beginning to make sense.

CHAPTER THIRTEEN

THEY WERE MARRIED a few days later, in the quaint chapel in the grounds of the *castello*. Saskia wore a luxurious cashmere dress of whisper-grey, her hair coiled artfully on her head and a handpicked bouquet of calla lilies in her hands, and her heart beat a tattoo on the inside of her chest.

She recited her vows in front of him, trying not to think too much about the words themselves, or how they related to her. And certainly trying not to listen too closely to the promises Malachi was making, in a voice so deep and clear that it had every hair on her body standing to attention.

What would it feel like to have this man standing in front of her and saying those words because he truly loved her and wanted to be with her? And not just because she was the mother of his unborn child?

She could imagine that if she listened, if she'd imagined those words truly were for her, then she would be swept up in the magic of it. She already very nearly had been.

Malachi had a way of looking at her that made her feel cherished. Wanted. *Loved.* She had to keep reminding herself that it was the baby he felt all those emotions for. Not her.

It wasn't real.

But she wanted it to be. Far more than she had any right to do.

When it was time to kiss the bride she expected some brief peck on the cheek, in line with the way he'd kept away from her these last few weeks. So when he gathered her to him, his hand gently smoothing a stray lock of hair from her face, then pressed his lips to hers in a way which held such unspoken emotion and promise, she was sure she'd crack apart right then and there.

She wanted him with an intensity that threatened to overwhelm her.

She *loved* him.

There was no other word for it. And it hurt beyond reason that he didn't feel the same way. That he would never feel that way.

No wonder she'd been setting herself impossible standards—it had protected her heart. Andy's betrayal hadn't even come close to causing her the pain she felt knowing that she loved the one man who could never love her back.

And after they'd returned to the *castello*, and the meal that Imelda had prepared for them with such love, she was ready when Malachi withdrew some time later, closeting himself in his study to throw himself into work—and keep away from her.

Saskia was sitting in front of the fire in her favourite room in the *castello*. The library. She'd read so many books over the past few weeks and tried out every chair, every window seat, every couch in the room. Suddenly, Malachi strode through the doors, seeming to fill the room with white heat in an instant.

She lowered the book onto her lap carefully and folded her hands, trying not to let them shake with the delicious surprise of it. He had been avoiding her for the last fortnight, holed up in his office, furiously working on some new business deal or other. She was certain that, had it not been for the snowstorms which had battered the region, he would have gone weeks ago, leaving her alone in the *castello* but for the kind and bustling Imelda.

'The doctor has told me that you're doing much better,' he announced, without preamble.

Saskia looked up at him. She'd been begging him for a month now to leave the *castello*, but he'd refused to provide a vehicle and told her the roads were too treacherous for her to go alone. He'd made his concern for her health and that of their baby clear.

Which only made her wonder all the more about what Malachi wanted now.

Was he suggesting that she would be able to return home to the UK? Back to London? Possibly even back to work at the hospital? They would surely welcome her. In all likelihood they'd be short of staff.

'Much better. It seems this rest has been just what I needed. The baby is fine and developing well.'

He dipped his head curtly. 'I thought you might be tired of being cooped up indoors.'

This *was* a surprise.

'I am—as I'm sure I've told you many times,' she agreed. 'Very tired of it.'

'Then make sure you have warm clothes and a decent coat. We're heading out.'

It took her a moment to gather her skittering thoughts. 'Where?'

'You'll see.'

Before she could ask any more questions he spun on his heel and marched straight back out of the library.

For two weeks he had practically ignored her presence here in the *castello*. Did he really think that he could click his fingers now and she would go running?

Well, he could just think again.

She told herself that her racing heart was crossness, not anticipation.

Ten minutes later, the door opened again.

'Since you didn't appear to be moving, I took the liberty of bringing you a thick jumper and your coat. You look warm enough otherwise.'

Saskia stared at him. 'You went into my room? You went through my clothes?'

And her outrage had nothing to do with the fact that in those drawers lurked the laciest scraps of material, which she still didn't even understand why she'd packed.

It was as if a traitorous part of her had imagined a stay in Malachi's *castello* would lead to more…*intimate* pursuits.

'You appeared to need the assistance.' He raised one eyebrow unapologetically. 'Perhaps the doctor was mistaken when he thought you were better.'

She had the vague impression that she was baring her teeth at him. But it was either that or crumple with shame. 'You had no right,' she breathed.

'What kind of a husband would I be if I didn't help the mother of my unborn baby?'

'And here was I thinking that you'd been avoiding me these past couple of weeks—since our wedding that no one seems to know about. Are you hiding me away out of shame?'

Shockingly, Malachi flinched, as if she had scored a direct hit. As though he felt guilty for it.

He regrouped quickly. 'I was trying to be considerate by affording you space.'

'Is that really what you were doing, Malachi?' she asked softly.

And then she seemed to score an even heavier hit as his gaze locked with hers.

His lips pressed into a thin, vaguely appalled line. 'Put your coat on,' he commanded at last. 'We're leaving.'

Then, once again, he exited the room, this time leaving her to scurry behind him.

'Are you serious?'

Saskia stopped at the doors of the *castello*, staring down the steps to the horse-drawn sleigh below. The storms had abated and the late-afternoon winter sun was out, bouncing and shining off the snow. A true wonderland.

'I thought a sleigh ride through the valley might be a nice way for you to get out and get some fresh air.'

'A sleigh ride?'

'Tonight is a celebration and they put on a fireworks display as part of Tuscany's many winter fire festivals.'

A sleigh ride and fireworks? Under other circumstances, it might have even sounded romantic. Still, it would be a glorious way for her to get out. Aside from the brief walks snatched in between blustery snowfalls, she felt as though she'd been cooped up indoors for ever.

But with Malachi?

Pressed up against him in the back of the sleigh, under that blanket she could see covering the back seat? Was that really a good idea?

'With you?'

'That was the idea.' His mouth twitched upwards.

Her head screamed *No!* Yet the thrill that rippled through her body cried *Why not?* And in the end it was her body that won out.

Saskia descended the stone steps as gracefully as she could, pretending it didn't sear right through her when she took his proffered hand and allowed him to help her into the sleigh. She feigned nonchalance when he climbed up behind her, settling down so closely that she was certain the emotions raging inside her were going to cause her entire body to implode with tension.

And then he put his arm around her and drew her into him, and it was like a thousand tiny detonations going off inside her chest.

'So, you told me you've always wanted to visit the Amiata?' he said. 'What do you know about it?'

'I know it's an extinct volcano, and also one of the highest mountains in Tuscany. And I know it has lava domes rather than a volcanic crater.'

'Did you know that its last recorded volcanic

activity was between two hundred and three hundred thousand years ago?' he asked, his voice rumbling low around her. 'And that it also puts the *hot* into the hot springs of Tuscany?'

And elsewhere, if she was being honest.

'I did know that, actually. I understand that the water which filters deep down comes into contact with the magma and then trickles its way up through crevices in the Earth's crust.'

It was all she could do to keep her head focussed on the conversation and not the feel of Malachi's body, all heat and steel, against hers.

'Some of it trickles,' he concurred. 'But some of it gushes up at over five hundred litres per second, like the thermal baths at Saturnia.'

'I've always wanted to visit them!' Saskia gasped, unable to stop herself.

'Maybe we can. One day. When you aren't pregnant.'

One day?

Something danced through her at the idea of Malachi thinking into the future, even as logic told her that she was a fool for reading too much into such a throwaway comment.

'So,' she forced a light, even merry note into her voice, 'tell me more about these fire festivals you mentioned before.'

'You've never heard about them?'

'I haven't, as it happens.'

It was as though the moment of openness had

created a spark of connection. A strange current seemed to weave around them, even as Saskia berated herself for her foolishness.

'There are fire festivals throughout Tuscany all year round. There are torchlight—or Fiacco-lata—festivals, bonfires, fireworks, and candle-light or paper lantern festivals where kids use peashooters to try to set fire to the coloured lanterns.'

'So is that where we're going now?'

'Not tonight,' he laughed, and it should surely worry her that the sound made her whole body heat up, like a shot of the strongest 192-proof Spirytus.

'Rificolona is in September, in Florence,' he explained. 'Tonight is a traditional bonfire festival. A symbolic reminder of an ancient rivalry between two neighbourhoods in the village. There will be stalls, and games, and a small fireworks display and each side competes to have the biggest and best bonfire.'

'And what does the winner receive?'

She felt drawn in already. Something about the passion in Malachi's voice made her realise that this was more than just a festival to him. This was where he loved to be. This was 'home'.

'The reward isn't something you can touch, or take home to display on a mantelshelf.' He smiled. 'It's far more than that. The winning

neighbourhood will have the most successful
year in terms of health, of happiness, of love.'

'Oh.'

'Last year, the winners were the south side
neighbourhood,' Malachi said gruffly. 'The following month two young couples who had each
had failed IVF treatment, and who had both
given up hope for babies of their own, fell pregnant within a week of each other. A couple of
months ago the village welcomed healthy, happy
Sofia Lombardi and Marco Alfonsi.'

'Oh,' Saskia managed, her throat suddenly inexplicably thick. Full. 'It sounds…like something
worth building the best bonfire for.'

'Yes. I believe it does.'

Perhaps it was the twilight that started to fall
around them shortly after their journey began.
Maybe it was the pretty swinging lanterns on the
sleigh and the soft jingling of the bells. Possibly
it was the magic of the horse-drawn ride itself.
Whatever it was, Saskia found herself relaxing
into the moment, letting her body ease against
Malachi's as he told her the names of each moun-
tain in the range, how the nature reserve in the
valley was one of over one hundred in the Tuscany area, and which of the buildings made up
part of the Medici villas.

He was knowledgeable and witty, sharing an-
ecdotes and unusual facts with her to make the
sleigh ride all the more interesting. She couldn't

help but wonder what marriage—*real* marriage—to this man might be like. He would certainly make learning fun for any child...

For *their* child.

By the time an hour was over her head was a jumble of conflicting emotions, and she barely realised they were heading back towards the local village, which she had longed to visit every time she'd looked out of her window and down the valley.

The fireworks were starting, and she was just settling back to enjoy them when a scream and a shout went up. Before Saskia knew what was happening, Malachi had withdrawn his arm from around her and was vaulting down off the sleigh. She began to throw the blanket off herself.

'What are you doing?' he demanded.

'Coming with you. If someone has been injured then I'm the best person to be there, don't you think?'

'No, I *don't* think,' he barked. 'Stay where you are! That isn't a request, Saskia. I'll be back in a moment.'

Then he was gone, racing into the melee with all the speed and power of a hundred-metre sprinter.

She hesitated, thought twice, then jumped down and followed him at an altogether slower pace.

The reason for the shout became clear quite

quickly. A young boy, wanting to get in on the thrill of the night, had tried to set off his own firework—only for it to go off when he had still been too close.

There was someone running towards the young boy with a bucket of ice, and without thinking Saskia reacted. She grabbed a couple of bottles of water from a nearby food stand and started to run.

'No, wait. Not ice. Um…*non usare il ghiaccio*.' She hurried across the field, aware that Malachi had spun around and was now right beside her, translating in fast, possibly flawless, Italian.

'I told you to wait in the sleigh,' he snapped.

'And I told *you* that if there was a medical emergency then I was better off coming with you,' she replied smoothly. 'But I know you're only concerned, so I'll forgive you trying to boss me around.'

He hauled off his coat and threw it around her shoulders, growling, but somehow it only made her smile, and she felt a warmth seeping through her despite the cold night air.

'Tell them ice can damage tissues and increase the risk of infection. They're better off with cool running water.'

Malachi duly translated, and Saskia wasn't sure if it was her instructions or merely his presence which had them instantly obeying.

She reached the casualty—a young boy likely around ten years old.

'Can I look?' She smiled gently. *'Posso... guardare?'*

The burn was on his forearm, quite large and already red and swelling, and she threw one bottle of water to Malachi to open whilst she opened the other and began pouring it over his wound. But it was the boy's pale, cold skin and rapid, shallow breathing which concerned her.

'Come ti chiami?'

'Andreas,' a young, worried-looking girl answered. 'His name is Andreas. I am Giulia... *sorella*? Sister?'

'His sister, yes,' Saskia smiled. *'Ciao*, Giulia, I'm here to take care of your brother.'

'Grazie.'

*'E...tuoi...*your parents...are they here?' She cast an apologetic glance at Malachi as she reverted to English, her limited grasp of Italian spent.

He translated quickly, only for Giulia to shake her head and begin speaking in Italian too fast for Saskia even to begin to understand. Then the girl got up and pushed through the crowd.

'There's only their mother. She's working in the town tonight—Giulia is going to try to get hold of her now.'

'Andreas is showing signs of shock,' she murmured to Malachi. 'He really needs to get to hospital. Can you carry him into that house over there? We must keep his wound under running water, but we also need to get him on his back and elevate his legs, to increase blood flow to his head and heart.'

Even as Malachi scooped the boy up, translating her instructions in that calm, firm way of his, Saskia began emptying another bottle of water over the boy's arm, moving his clothing out of the way after ensuring nothing was stuck to the wound.

The owner of the house ran ahead, flicking all the lights on and holding doors open, and a small crowd flanked them, murmuring with concern but apparently happy to follow Saskia's instructions.

Before long the boy was lying on the floor in the bathroom, his arm under the cool flow from a handheld showerhead, his legs elevated by a small upturned laundry basket, his body covered with a blanket.

'How long does he need to stay like this?' asked Malachi.

'I'll check it after ten minutes or so. I could probably use some cling film to cover the burn. Something that will keep it clear of infection but isn't fluffy.'

'So not cotton wool?' He eyed the bag that had been handed to him by the homeowner.

'No—exactly,' Saskia confirmed. 'But if it comes to it we can tip out the cotton balls and use the bag itself. I'd just prefer something off a roll, so I know it's really clean.'

'I'll go and ask what they have. You'll be okay?'

'We'll be fine.' She turned to the little boy. '*Bene*, Andreas?'

He nodded stiffly, already looking a little less clammy.

She sat with him, keeping him under close observation even as the villagers, following her instructions as relayed via Malachi, kept talking to the young lad and soothing him.

It felt like only seconds since he'd left for the supplies she'd suggested, but already he was back, and she had to admit that his improvisation of a fresh roll of freezer bags was well chosen.

'I brought a variety of painkillers, too. I wasn't sure what was best.'

Saskia quickly sifted through them. 'These or these,' she confirmed. 'Not those.'

Malachi relayed the information to the homeowner before turning back to her.

'The ambulance is nearly here. It will take him to the local clinic, eight miles away, so I think it's best you do whatever you think needs doing before we transfer him.'

'Thanks.' Saskia nodded, his trust in her gloriously buoying. 'Can you take this whilst I wrap his arm?'

They worked well together, a surprisingly good team. Malachi seemed intuitive, anticipating what she would need next, and he chatted to the boy to keep him happy about what was going on.

By the time they'd finished, and Andreas had been safely transferred to the ambulance, he looked much more comfortable and Saskia knew she had been accepted by the community.

Then, as she slipped Malachi's coat off her shoulders because he must be cold, she heard their gasps and realised they hadn't known she was pregnant. Suddenly they were the centre of attention again, with everyone rushing to congratulate them—congratulate Malachi.

A thrill ran through Saskia at the way he reacted—as though they were a real couple. So much so that she almost even fooled herself.

For a moment she wondered why she was holding out for some great passion. Why she was pretending she believed in the shining Hollywood example of her parents' great love affair. Especially when she knew the dark, cruel truth.

Maybe Malachi was right. Maybe what they

had—chemistry and sexual passion, with a healthy dose of mutual respect—was enough.

Perhaps when they got back to the castle she ought to tell him.

'Thank you,' she whispered quietly, as he helped her down from the sleigh and walked with her over the grass to the *castello*.

'What? For today?'

'For today…' She tilted her head. 'And for the last few months. I know you've only been trying to help and I haven't made things easier.'

'No, you haven't,' he agreed, but there was no heat to his words. 'Why is that, Saskia?'

'I don't know,' she admitted. 'Perhaps I thought I wanted my child to have more than just two people who married because they thought it was the right thing to do.'

'And there's something wrong with doing the right thing?'

'I don't know. I think I wanted us to know love, and warmth, and *family*. The things the world believes I had. The things you never had. And, more than that, Malachi, I think *I* needed to have that. I wanted more than just a marriage of convenience. I guess I'd had enough of my parents, or Andy, or whoever and I just wanted to have someone who really *wanted* to be with me.'

She stopped, her chest aching as she thought about her parents.

'Actually, scratch that. I want someone who *has* to be with me. Who can't breathe without me. Who can't breathe without our baby. Who doesn't *want* to breathe without us.'

'I told you—that's a movie screen fantasy,' he bit out. 'That doesn't exist.'

'Maybe it doesn't. But, then again, maybe you're wrong and it does exist,' she countered softly, glancing down at her belly as she laid one protective hand over it. 'I think it might do, even if it isn't what I've been pretending to myself it is. Even if what my parents had wasn't it after all.'

He wasn't sure what he was doing. One moment he was trying to clench his fingers, just so that he didn't give in to the itch to reach for her again. The next he was kissing her.

His hands cupped her face as he practically drank her in, as if she was the most intoxicating thing he'd ever tasted.

Perhaps she was. But he didn't care. He didn't want to stop.

He might have kissed her for hours. Days. Exploring her, reacquainting himself with her and delighting in her. Even when they finally surfaced he found he couldn't let her go, and she sighed a deep shuddery breath, her lips still brushing his cheek.

'What are you doing, Malachi?'

He wasn't sure he even knew. 'You accused

me of being controlled, reserved, and you told me you didn't want that.'

'So…' She paused. 'This is you being…impulsive?'

'Yes.'

He dropped another kiss on her shoulder and felt another quiver cascade through her.

'You being reckless?'

'Indeed.'

Another kiss. Another tremor.

'You being…unsuppressed?'

'It *was*,' he growled wryly. And he lamented the loss of the kiss even as his voice vibrated through her. 'Until *you* decided to overanalyse it.'

'I apologise!' Saskia chuckled softly. 'I just—'

'That's enough. Stop talking.' He cut her off, ruthlessly and effectively, his mouth claiming hers. Stamping his authority all over her.

And he found that Saskia didn't seem to mind a bit.

She gave herself up to his touch. She matched it greedy stroke for greedy stroke. She tasted magnificent, better even than he remembered, and he revelled in every second of it. She slid her arms around his neck and he wasn't sure whether he hauled her closer or whether she pressed herself to him.

Possibly both.

And then he slid one hard, lean thigh between her legs, pressing against her core, making her rock against him. But when she did he found he couldn't get close enough. Her burgeoning bump was in the way.

And judging by the small sound of surprise she made, Saskia had felt it, too.

Instantly, Malachi set her away.

'No, I'm fine—I'm fine,' she protested, moving closer.

'Are you?'

He looked at her with concern until she defused the situation with a laugh.

'I'm not *that* big. It was just unexpected, that's all. I'm not used to it.'

'Really?'

Resisting her attempt to step closer again, he kept his hands on her hips, holding her away.

Suddenly he saw unease lance through her.

'Or is it that you don't find me appealing like this?' she asked.

'Say that again?' he said.

His expression darkened but she didn't know what that meant. Had she been reading him incorrectly all this time? Had he made himself absent these last two weeks not because he didn't want to give in to the attraction they'd once shared, but because he no longer found her attractive?

Saskia hated herself. She didn't consider herself catwalk-model-esque, but nor had she ever needed to be flattered or constantly built up. She had always prided herself on being self-assured—she was who she was, and it was entirely up to other people whether they decided to take it or leave it.

Yet now, suddenly, with Malachi, she found herself wondering how she measured up. What had his past lovers been like? How would her swelling body compare?

'You're not compelled to,' she rambled on, unable to stop herself. But this wasn't her. At least it wasn't who she wanted to be. All needy and timid.

'You can't seriously be asking me that question?'

He sounded…*angry*? Somehow—and Saskia had no idea how—she managed to tilt her head up and look him in the eye, to move away from this mousy stranger who inhabited her body.

'I would rather know.' She was going for confident, but she just sounded sharp.

Malachi cursed. Low, almost under his breath, but she heard it nonetheless.

'Strip,' he commanded.

Had she heard that right?

'Pardon?'

'Strip.'

His voice rasped over her, abrading her from the inside out. In an instant the fire smouldering within her kicked back into life.

'And then I shall demonstrate exactly how beautiful I think you are. Even more so now.'

It was all the reassurance Saskia needed. The hunger in his tone ignited her, like a match to petrol. Without taking another step towards him she locked her gaze with his, the blood pounding through her veins as she slid off her jumper. Taking her time, she began unbuttoning her shirt, and as Malachi inhaled sharply, heat spiralled through her. A corkscrew of desire headed straight for her core. His eyes gleamed and she allowed it to slide down her shoulders before letting it fall to a puddle at her feet.

But if she'd thought he would fall at her feet, too, she'd been sorely mistaken. The truth hit her as if she'd been doused with a bucket of ice water. His eyes had stopped at her middle. Right where the obvious swell of her abdomen was showing.

And his hard gaze wasn't one of pride or tenderness.

'Malachi—' she began, not knowing what to say.

'You were right,' he cut in harshly. 'This isn't a good idea.'

Pain sliced through her. He was rejecting her—but, more than that, he was rejecting her baby.

Their baby.

Even though she'd known all along what kind

of a man Malachi was—a businessman, not a family man—it didn't just hurt. It constricted her heart. As if he'd just thrust his fist inside her chest and was squeezing it.

She couldn't move. Couldn't even breathe. They both stood immobile, staring at each other, and the earth might as well have been splintering apart, fracturing, as a whole chasm opened up between them.

Abruptly, without a word, Malachi turned and strode out of the room.

And the soft closing of the door behind him echoed in Saskia's head, louder and with more finality than the last time he'd walked out on her, back at his penthouse a few months earlier.

Malachi had no idea where he was going. He'd marched around the *castello* before his brain had even registered where his body was taking him.
What the hell had he been thinking?
Somehow she had imprinted on him when he hadn't been looking. So much for his assertion that marriage to Saskia was the *right and proper* thing to do, given the circumstances.

Deep down, he knew that was if not a lie, then surely only the half of it.

Deep down, he recognised that it wasn't completely honourable, the reason why he wanted Saskia as his bride; the truth was far worse.

Deep down, he understood that Saskia felt it, too.

Which made it all the more dangerous for them to be here in this *castello* in the middle of winter, together.

He couldn't risk staying. He wasn't sure he could trust himself around her.

The only thing he had to give her was his honour, his integrity. He couldn't give her the grand love she wanted but he had promised to protect her.

And their baby.

And so far he had failed at both things.

If anything had happened to his unborn baby because he had given in to this dark, intense… *thing* that twisted inside him, that craved her so desperately, he would never have forgiven himself.

It was a mistake to have married her, and it was a mistake to have brought her here.

She'd told him that ages ago, but he'd thought he knew better.

Turned out he wasn't the man he'd thought he was.

He certainly wasn't the man Saskia—or his baby—deserved.

CHAPTER FOURTEEN

'WHAT HAVE YOU got for me, ladies?' Saskia plastered a smile onto her face, as if that could convince the world that she was feeling happy inside.

Maybe one day she would finally be over Malachi Gunn enough to convince herself of the fact, too.

'Here she is—Moorlands General's little trooper.'

'Well, thank you, Babette,' she forced out, despite knowing perfectly well it hadn't been a compliment.

It never was. And it had been a long enough shift as it was, but Babette's constant sniping hadn't made things any easier. At least she would be out of here in less than an hour. Or should be, anyway.

'What have we got, Maggie?' She turned to the other nurse instead.

'Stella Jones, four years old, nasal foreign body. Previous intervention by parents and local

GP, but his attempt to retrieve it only pushed the object further inside.'

'You won't be able to do anything,' Babette commented disparagingly. 'The family have been sent here for local anaesthetic before removal.'

Saskia very nearly bit her tongue—literally.

'I'll take a look anyway.'

'It's a waste of time.'

'Strangely enough, it's my job,' Saskia countered, taking a moment to peruse the notes in peace before heading towards the cubicle.

'Hello, Mrs Jones. I'm Saskia, and you must be…wait…let me guess… Stella.'

Stella cast her a woebegone look whilst her mother practically slumped with relief.

'Stella stuck a bead up her nose a couple of days ago. I tried to get it out, and so did our doctor, but it just won't come down.'

'Stella, would you mind if I had a little look?' Saskia used her softest voice.

Stella wriggled up the bed until her back was wedged into the corner of the wall and shook her head mutinously.

'I'm on her naughty list, too—for bringing her to all these doctors,' the mother offered a weak smile.

'It's a thankless task being a parent, isn't it?' Saskia sympathised, before cranking her smile up a notch and turning back to Stella. 'Has it been hurting a lot, sweetie?'

She was rewarded with a vigorous nod.

The notes said that the object wasn't visible on an anterior rhinoscopy, but she would like to see for herself.

'If I promise I won't try to get it out, would you just let me have a little look? I could pinkie swear?'

The little girl eyed her sceptically for what felt like an age.

'Please let the doctor look, flower,' Mrs Jones cajoled. 'We can't leave it up there—it will make you really ill.'

Stella turned to her mother and shook her head again, but this time it was a little less emphatic. Then she edged across the bed for a cuddle.

Not a bad sign, Saskia considered. It might take a little more careful treading and negotiation, but this might not take as long as she'd initially feared.

'What happened with the GP?' she asked the mother, making no move to approach Stella yet.

'What happened? Well, he looked up her nose and at first he could see the bead, so he tried to get it out with tweezers, but he couldn't. I think he might have pushed it up deeper, because afterwards he wasn't sure he could see it any more, but Stella wouldn't keep still so he couldn't get a proper look.'

'Okay, I see. So—what about this, sweetie?' Saskia kept her back against her seat as she faced the little girl again. 'I'll have a little look—just a look, no trying to get the bead out—and then, if I can see it, maybe Mummy can give you a big kiss and that might help to get the bead out for you.'

'A big kiss?' Stella's mother looked puzzled.

'It's called "the parent's kiss"—basically, it's something a trusted parent or adult can do for a young child, to help simulate the effect of a sneeze or a gentle nose-blow.'

'Will it really work?'

'It might. Especially with it being a small, smooth bead that Stella has put up there. It's certainly worth trying before we move on to anything more invasive. But I have to know if I can even see the object first.'

'Stella, flower, if you let the doctor check your nose, I think I might be able to get you that little puppy toy you liked.'

Stella perked up, so Saskia tried a stage whisper.

'I can definitely tell Mummy that you deserve a puppy toy if you're so brave.'

Within ten minutes, and after a little more cajoling, Saskia had the answer she needed, and now Stella was sitting upright on a chair, her back pressed against the fabric, and her mother was sitting, white-faced, in front of her.

'So, Stella, you're going to open your mouth

just a little. Mum, you'll need to use your own mouth to make a seal around your daughter's. You'll press your thumb against the unobstructed nostril and then you'll exhale in a short, sharp puff.'

'Just one?'

'We can repeat the process up to five times, but just one at a time. When you're ready, go ahead.'

'How tightly do I press my thumb on her nostril?'

'Tightly enough to stop the air escaping. The more air that shoots down the obstructed nostril, the more chance it has to dislodge the bead.'

'Oh, I see.' Mrs Jones nodded suddenly. 'Okay. So... I just do it?'

'When you're ready.'

As the mother adjusted her grip on her daughter, Stella squirmed.

Saskia knelt down next to her. 'Don't worry sweetie,' she soothed. 'It's just going to be like a big kiss from Mummy. And the stiller you can stay, the more chance the bead will come out. And I would *love* that, because I don't want to have to try and get it with any of my instruments, and I don't think you want that either, do you?'

Another wild head-shake.

'Good,' encouraged Saskia. 'So, shall we let Mummy have a go at trying to help?'

A tentative nod.

'Clever girl. Okay, be brave and think of that toy puppy. You can look at me, if you like. I do a great Donald Duck impression.'

'Good call, Saskia,' Maggie commented as they finished discharging a much happier Stella. 'Don't you think, Babette?'

Babette sniffed, and Saskia supressed a ripple of irritation. How long would she have to be practising as a doctor before she didn't let Babette get to her? Why did she even care?

'I guess...' Babette shrugged, giving the impression that it was anything but good. 'Hadn't you better be leaving soon, anyway? You don't want to turn up to the gala looking like *that*.'

'What gala?' Saskia regretted the question even as it was leaving her mouth.

'The Valentine's Day gala.' Babette stopped, a gleam instantly chasing the dullness from her expression. 'You don't know what I'm talking about, do you?'

Saskia didn't want to lie. But then, she didn't want to give Babette the upper hand, either.

'I know. I just forgot.' She managed to remain impressively nonchalant. 'I've got a prior engagement.'

'With a tub of ice cream and your pyjamas?' Babette snorted, clearly delighted with the turn of events. 'What could be more important than supporting your husband—the father of your unborn baby—in his biggest charity dinner to date?'

There was no pretending now. Not on either side. Babette was practically purring as she licked the proverbial cream from her whiskers, whilst Saskia felt so winded she was astonished she wasn't on her back on the cold floor of the corridor, staring up at the stark white ceiling.

'Andy has been reminding me about it for months. Making sure I've got everything I need. New dress, sexy heels, gorgeous jewellery...'

The woman was really laying it on thickly now. Saskia bared her teeth and hoped it would pass for a cold smile.

'He really does take care of me—but you know how that feels, don't you, Saskia? Then again...maybe you don't. I *do* hope I haven't caused any offence.'

Saskia had no idea how she managed to open her mouth, let alone speak. She certainly didn't recognise the airy, almost amused voice that came out of it.

'Oh, don't you worry about me, Babette. Now that I'm out of a toxic relationship and in a much more mature one I don't take offence so easily. It's amazing what a secure partnership does for a person.'

'So secure that you didn't even know about the Valentine's gala the Gunn brothers are holding in order to raise money for their precious charity Careful Playing?' Babette shot back.

But Saskia noticed that the woman didn't sound quite as confident as she had before.

She ramped her smile up a notch. 'Care to Play.'

'Play what?' Babette snapped, now clearly rattled. 'I'm not playing at anything.'

Oh, I think you are.

'Malachi's charity is called Care to Play. It provides a safe centre for young carers to just be kids for a few hours and forget their usual responsibilities. I've volunteered there several times, but Malachi wanted me to ease back until the baby is born.'

That much, at least, was true.

'Maybe he just doesn't want you around,' sneered Babette, having finally dispensed with any attempt at veiling her snipes. 'Have you ever thought that perhaps he doesn't *want* you sticking your nose into other areas of his life, and concern about your pregnancy is just a convenient excuse?'

It was galling how closely her words seemed to mirror all of Saskia's deepest fears. It just proved what a viper the woman was.

But Saskia wasn't about to let her know how acutely her words cut. 'Surely you're not suggesting that Malachi's concern for our baby isn't genuine?' She shook her head, managing to appear genuinely bemused.

'No. I was suggesting—'

'Oh, well, that's a relief,' Saskia cut in swiftly, realising she'd just been handed a way to use Babette's earlier words against her. 'I could only imagine how *offended* he would be if he thought what I just did.'

'What? No...'

But Saskia was already striding down the corridor as fast as she could, head held deliberately high, before Babette could regain her footing and hit her with a typically cutting comeback.

However, the reality was that any sense of victory she was feeling in that moment was fleeting. Any moment now Babette's remarks were going to circle back in her head, echoing all the fears she'd been trying to push aside for what felt like for ever.

Malachi hadn't invited her to the gala tonight. He hadn't even told her about it. His life was so neat, so ordered, with each part of it separate from the others. His work life, his charity, his personal life...

Not one seemed to cross the divide between one and another. Not even her.

Especially not her.

Sadness, and something else she couldn't—*wouldn't?*—put a name to, trickled through her.

They lived together, they were husband and

wife, and they were expecting a baby together. Yet in all other areas they might as well be complete strangers.

Saskia didn't know whether that was her fault or Malachi's. She only knew that one of them was going to have to make the first move if they wanted to resolve it.

So why not her?

And why not tonight?

'What the hell do you think you're doing here?'

He gripped her elbow tightly, manoeuvring her off the floor.

It was all Saskia could do to hide her surprise and school her features into some semblance of a smile as he ushered her firmly through the throng.

'I'm here to support you,' she managed in a low voice, once they were out of the way of the main crowd. 'To support your charity.'

He expelled air slowly through his teeth, making a hissing sound.

'You're not needed, Saskia. Go home.'

'On Valentine's Day? At a ball for couples?'

'You're not needed, Saskia,' he repeated, his teeth gritted.

'But I *want* to be here.'

She would have thought that his expression couldn't darken any further, yet somehow it managed it.

'You have no place here.'

A closeness tightened around her. She tried to fight it.

'I'm your wife…' The whispered plea fell from her lips, but it didn't seem to soften the granite-faced Malachi towards her at all. If anything, he appeared all the more impenetrable.

'So stay in that part of my life. I don't want you in this part.'

She wasn't hearing him right. She couldn't be.

Panic threatened to overtake her.

'You can't pigeonhole your life like that.'

'I can. I do. My business life and my charity work have always been two distinct areas of my life. They don't mix and they don't need to. Why should our crafted marriage be any different?'

'Because…it *is*,' she cried helplessly. 'Because *we're* different. Whatever this was meant to be at the start, it's real now, and we're having a baby together. Or is our baby not real to you any more? Is she not welcome in your life?'

He advanced on her. So close that she couldn't stop herself from backing up, right into the wall behind her. It reminded her of that night back in his apartment at Christmas time. Except this time when he lifted his arms and placed his hands on either side of her head it felt more like a cage than ever.

'Our baby is the *only* real thing about all this,' he said.

His voice was rasping. Much too rough for her to mistake the emotion in it. Not that she was about to.

'And she will always be welcome in my life. *All* areas of my life. And she will be loved more than you can imagine.'

'And yet here I am, the mother of that child, and you don't even want me dipping a toe into the waters of any other part of your life.'

She barely recognised her own voice—it was loaded with something she couldn't quite identify. Or didn't want to.

'You're a master at compartmentalising your life, aren't you?'

She realised her voice was too sharp, too high, but she couldn't stop it. And his expression was so bleak, so haunted, that it scraped inside her. Like a scalpel blade to her chest wall. And when he spoke, in that distant, cold tone, she half expected her skin to freeze and blacken with frostbite.

'You say it like it's a bad thing. Besides, I would have thought that was something you would welcome. After all, it benefits you, too.'

'How does it remotely *benefit* me?' she exploded.

'We aren't a couple, Saskia. We never were. I was your rebound and then you fell pregnant. But I was never the man you were in love with.'

And suddenly everything fell into place.

The simple truth roared through Saskia and she wanted to scream, and laugh, and sob—all at the same time.

He loved her. This beautiful, impossible, impenetrable man loved her—perhaps as much as she loved him.

He just didn't know it yet.

She lifted her hand, tentatively at first, and touched it to his chest, taking heart when he didn't pull away as she'd feared he would.

'You were never just my rebound, Malachi,' she whispered. 'You were always more than that.'

She heard a beat of silence. The moment when he absorbed what she'd said. But she should have known it wouldn't be that easy.

'I don't believe you, *zvyozdochka*.'

Her heart kicked. He'd given himself away with just that one term of endearment, and now her spirit was beginning to soar.

She lifted her hand to cup his cheek. 'It's true. I might not have realised it before, but I know it now. In my entire life I've never done anything like have a one-night stand. I'd only ever been with one man…'

'Whom you loved,' he reminded her grimly. 'You told me as much that first night.'

'I was wrong,'

'You want me to believe that you didn't love him?' He eyed her sceptically.

'I did love him. At the time. Or at least I loved

what I thought we had. The fact that he cheated on me—and if we're being honest who knows if Babette was the only one?—means that he was never the man I thought he was. Ergo, I could never have loved him. Not really…'

She faltered, waiting for him to speak. But he didn't. Still, his gaze never left hers. She had no choice but to forge on.

'I think what I was in love with was the *idea* of what we had. But then I met you, and we had that crazy weekend. After that it was all you. You were the one I thought about. You were the one who threw out the questions and *what ifs* in my head. And then I discovered I was pregnant, and I think that was the excuse I'd been looking for to talk to you again. To see if maybe you'd thought about me, too.'

Silence stretched out between them. All Saskia could hear was ragged breathing. Hers? His? Probably both.

Abruptly Malachi pushed himself off the wall, taking a few steps back. Away from her. She almost reached out to stop him, but knew it would be a mistake.

'But you didn't come to talk to me,' he said. 'You didn't approach me at all. In fact, the first chance you had to see me you ran away from me. You recall that, of course?' He was challenging her. 'You aren't trying to rewrite history?'

'Yes, I recall that. We were in a consultation

room. I was at work. You were there for my patient and her family. And… And I had no idea how to tell you that I was pregnant.'

'That's pitiful, *zvyozdochka.*'

'You may be right.' She straightened her shoulders. 'But that doesn't make it any less true.'

His glower deepened. It couldn't be a good sign that he wouldn't even look at her. Instead, his glare was directed at some unseen spot on the wall behind her.

'I was frightened and I was lost. I wasn't sure if I could do it on my own. And then you made it so I didn't have to. When I went in for that emergency scan, when they discovered that our baby was…' She choked on the words, swallowed, then pushed on. 'You were there with me every single step. You made sure I knew we were going through it all together. And I love you for that.'

'You do *not* love me, *zvyozdochka,*' he countered angrily. 'If I am not mistaken, what you feel—what you have described—is gratitude. They are not the same thing.'

She was losing him. She could see it right in front of her eyes and she was wholly powerless to stop it.

Fresh panic bubbled up inside her. 'So now you presume to tell me what I feel?'

'When you're claiming things which cannot possibly be true, then, *yes.* I'm not the kind of man you want, Saskia. Haven't you told me that a thousand times? I do not show my emotions the way you want. I don't speak the words of love you want to hear. I won't give you the poetry and the flowers you seem to think are proof of love. You believe in all of that, yet I do not.'

'And I was wrong!' she exclaimed. 'I got caught up in the hurt of being betrayed and I lost sight of what it means to actually love someone. I thought I needed those big, romantic gestures. It turns out I don't. I just need truth and honesty. I just need *you*, Malachi.'

A storm was raging within him. She saw it blustering over every one of his features. Watched its unobstructed trail. Knew it left devastation in its wake.

'I'm not the right man for you,' he bit out, turning his back on her and moving towards the ballroom. 'I will always be there for our baby, but I don't want you in the other areas of my life. Go home, Saskia. You're free at last.'

'I don't want to be free.'

'And *I* don't want you here.'

As he walked away, swallowed up by the crowd and carried out of her sight, Saskia slumped back against the wall and marvelled at just how badly she'd managed to mess things up.

CHAPTER FIFTEEN

'OKAY, SO ROSIE is a ten-year-old female with a BMI of nineteen. She presented with abdominal pain and a diagnosis of non-complicated gall-stone was made. Elective laparoscopic cholecys-tectomy has been scheduled for today.'

Saskia listened as her colleague ran through the surgery planned for the young patient.

She wouldn't go to the surgery, and knew this briefing was for the benefit of the surgical in-terns in the room, but she appreciated knowing what her patient was about to face. It gave her a greater depth of understanding, especially when talking to her patients later about post-op care—although of course the surgeon would have run through everything with the family.

'We'll place her supine, in a reverse position, at a thirty-degree angle, making a ten-millimetre incision at the umbilicus and pneumoperitoneum positions...'

Besides, work had always been her saviour when times were rough. She could always trust her job to refocus her brain and show her what really mattered. But this time was different. This time—even though she would never let her patients down or become distracted when it mattered—she couldn't shake Malachi, or the hold he seemed to have over her.

'And inserting two percutaneous atraumatic graspers into the abdomen via small incisions on the right side and on the mid-clavicular line...'

Her mind wandered to Rosie's parents. For the longest time she'd thought that Kevin, her father, was less concerned about his daughter, leaving her mother to ask the questions and try to understand what was going on with their daughter.

'The cystic duct and artery will be clipped, and the gallbladder extracted through the umbilical porthole...'

Perhaps she should have known better. She'd been a doctor long enough. But when she'd seen him take the surgeon's hand and heard him speak, low and sure, she'd realised that he didn't *need* to say much. He showed who he was, how supportive he was, by his actions, and in the way he didn't try to control the situation, letting his wife ask all the questions she needed whilst he absorbed everything, ready to talk through it with her when they were alone. A constant tower of support for both his wife and daughter.

Much like Malachi had been for her. And for their own baby.

Why had she thought she needed words and promises from him? Instead, he showed her who he was by every action and every deed.

When she'd needed him—when there had been complications with their baby—he had been there instantly. Always. Never leaving her side, and never letting her feel she was alone.

Because he *loved* her.

She'd been waiting and waiting, desperate to hear him say it, angry with herself, and him, when he hadn't. Waiting for beautiful, poetic words of love—more grandiose than anything Andy had ever said to her—which would prove to her that what was between her and Malachi was real.

She'd thought that after Andy's betrayal she'd need Malachi to go bigger and better than anything her ex-fiancé had ever done. Suddenly, she realised her mistake.

She was an idiot.

Because Malachi had done that.

She just hadn't been paying attention.

He had told her he loved her through every little thing he'd done for her. And for their baby. He just didn't know how to say the words.

But she could teach him, now that she understood him better.

Although she couldn't just go to him and tell him. After all the other things she'd said he would never believe her. She needed to prove it to him—to make that gesture she'd yearned for from him. She owed him that much.

Malachi slammed his fist down on the heavy, burr walnut desk.

He couldn't stand it any longer.

Thrusting his chair back from the desk, Malachi stood. He leaned over to activate the intercom to his secretary.

'I need you to arrange the helicopter for me, Geraldine.'

Geraldine's voice came clearly, crisply, through the speaker. 'Of course. Where to, sir?'

'Moorlands General,' he said decisively. 'Now, please.'

'Yes, sir.'

He was just about to terminate the communication when he heard her startled voice.

'Wait…you can't go in there…'

He'd reached for the switch to deactivate the privacy control on the glass wall when the door to his office burst open and Saskia strode boldly in.

'If you're looking for me, I'm right here.'

She placed her bag down and closed the door behind her, but he noticed that she didn't approach his desk. Perhaps not as bold as he'd first thought. The faint tremor in her hands suggested her confidence was a front.

Still, it had momentarily thrown him.

'So you are,' he bit out.

She looked well. Better than well. Her cheeks were red, as though she'd been walking outside in the cold, and her tousled hair made him think she'd recently tugged off one of those warm woolly hats she favoured. But it was the overcoat, pulled tight and cinched over the ever-expanding bump which took most of his attention.

Their baby.

'Well?' she demanded, as the quiet shimmered around the space.

'Sorry?'

'What were you coming to the hospital for?'

He glowered at her for a long moment before answering. 'To see you.'

'Well, it's good that I'm here, then.' Her eyes flashed, a frenetic expression whirling through them. 'I saved you the trouble.'

If he'd had to guess, he might have thought her nervous. Although the Saskia he knew had never been nervous about anything.

That said, she was bouncing around the room in a way he'd never seen her do before.

'Take a seat,' he suggested, fighting to slow his accelerating heartbeat.

'No.' She shook her head. 'Thanks. Are you ready to go?'

'To go where?'

'You'll see.'

And with that she practically danced out of the

room, leaving him with little choice but to grab his suit jacket and heavy woollen coat and follow.

He caught up with her just as the lift pinged, ready to take them down to the lobby. She was bobbing from one side to the other, shifting her weight as though she couldn't bear to be still for even an instant.

'Just slow down, Saskia. I haven't even called the car round to meet us outside.'

'No need.' She bustled them both out of the lift. 'We can walk.'

It was ridiculous, but her barely restrained excitement was infectious. Malachi found himself swept along in it even as he followed her.

'Walk where?'

'I told you—you'll see.'

He wanted to tell her that nothing had changed. That he still couldn't give her all the romance and sentiment she wanted. But he couldn't bring himself to speak; he didn't want to burst this little bubble of hers into which he could already feel himself being drawn.

It might be just an illusion, but it was one in which he wanted to revel—if only for a few more minutes.

And, besides, something had changed.

He'd realised that what he felt for her was—if not love itself—the closest thing he was ever going to get to it. She was like a fire, drawing him in from the cold. Her heat and her laughter had thawed him out when he'd thought he would never feel warm in his life.

It was why he let her lead him through the lobby now, watching her pull her woolly hat down over her curls before glancing over her shoulder to him and preceding him out of the revolving doors.

The streets were slick with rain, and he reached for her arm instinctively, wrapping it around his and ensuring that she didn't slip. And the wide smile she shot him kick-started some new alien sensation inside him.

It was as though she welcomed his care. As though she understood it for what it was.

Even if he wasn't quite sure that *he* did.

'Not far now,' she murmured, and he knew he wasn't imagining the nervous tremor in her tone, despite her overly bright smile.

It was only when they turned into the town hall that the wheels in his head finally began to spin.

'Saskia, what's going on?'

'Shh…nearly there,' she chided with a shaky laugh—but her voice cracked and betrayed her.

Moorlands Register Office.

'Did you know it's a leap year this year?'

Normally he would have known, but this past

week had blurred into itself so much that for once he had to stop and think.

'Is it?'

'It is,' she confirmed, her voice pitched higher than usual. 'And even though it might be the wrong month, I…thought I'd take advantage.'

'Advantage?' he echoed numbly.

'You were right all those months ago when you told me I was only holding out for a passionate love like my parents' because deep down I knew it had never really existed. It gave me the excuse I needed to keep people away—just like you do. Only at least you were more honest with yourself about what you were doing.'

'No, I don't think I was,' he refuted. The words were coming out without him intending them to. 'I think *you* were right. I thought I had come to terms with my childhood in a way Sol never had, but all I was doing was keeping it in front of me to…what did you say?…use as a shield.'

'So we've both taught each other something?'

Saskia smiled, and a shard of light pierced through him in an instant.

He'd grown so accustomed to the gloom in his world that he'd thought it was normal. Fine. But now he'd seen everything bathed in the vibrant colours of Saskia how was he ever to go back to that darkness?

'Why are we here, *zvyozdochka*?' he demanded, perhaps a little more sharply than he'd intended.

But she didn't blink—she just rewarded him with another of her dazzling smiles.

'You taught me that all the words of love and poetry I was holding out for don't bring much to the table after all. You taught me that actions really do speak louder than words, and you showed me how much you love me...*us*,' she corrected, smoothing a hand over her ever-growing abdomen. 'So now it's my turn.'

'This is unnecessary—' he began.

And yet he was doing nothing to move away from her. He certainly wasn't leaving. He was just standing there, breathing her in, trying to hold himself back from the insane need to cover her mouth with his and claim her as his.

His for ever.

'On the contrary, this is *entirely* necessary.' She cut across him. 'This is me proving to you that I don't need grand romantic gestures. I just need the little things that *mean* something.'

'Is that so?'

'It is.'

'And some grand, romantic gesture...?' His mouth twitched, but the gleam in his eyes reassured her.

'Ironic, isn't it?' she said merrily. 'Now, we're

already married, so I can't propose. But I *can* organise a renewal of vows. A chance for us to recommit to each other when we both know exactly what we're doing—and why. And a chance for us to do so in front of the two people we care about the most.'

Malachi knew, even before Sol and Anouk stepped around the corner, that his brother was going to be there. The one person he would have wanted to see him make a commitment to the woman of his dreams. It was as if she knew.

But maybe that was the point. Maybe Saskia really *did* know what he wanted and needed. She understood him, and she accepted him for what he was. And, after all, wasn't that the true measure of love?

'I think, Mrs Gunn,' he managed hoarsely, reaching out to haul her into his arms, bump and all, 'that I love you a little more every single day. And I want you in my life for the rest of time.'

'I'm pretty sure I can manage that,' she whispered, even as his mouth covered hers.

And her arms wrapped around him so tightly he hoped she would never let go.

Baby Gunn was born a mere week premature, with ten perfect toes and nine and a half perfect fingers. Her ankles still bore the scars of the amniotic bands, but Z-plasty would remedy that, just as a few months of night braces would correct the slight clubbing the bands had caused on her tiny chubby legs.

But to Saskia and Malachi their daughter looked beautiful. Their perfect baby, who had truly made their family whole.

* * * * *

*If you enjoyed this story, check out
these other great reads from
Charlotte Hawkes*

Unwrapping the Neurosurgeon's Heart
The Army Doc's Baby Secret
A Surgeon for the Single Mom
Christmas with Her Bodyguard

All available now!

The place was magnificent. Stone walls with battlements, sloping bases and arched windows made it impossible for her not to imagine the frescoed walls and coffered ceilings which must surely lie inside. And the building's beauty was matched only by the oaks and cypresses and ilex shrubs which framed it.

'It's a wonder you ever come back to London,' she murmured to him, wondering why it felt so instantly comfortable, familiar to her.

Like a *home*.

It was almost a relief that her words were whipped away, unheard, by the roar of the heli.

Together they made their way across the lawns, glistening white under a thin veil of snow, to the housekeeper, who was waiting at the door.

'I told you to stay inside in the warmth, Imelda,' Malachi admonished, and Saskia was shocked to see the little, rotund older lady, with a faint West Country accent, throwing her arms around him and kissing him soundly on each cheek.

'I stayed at the door, didn't I?' she teased. 'It's so good to have you back, Malachi.' Then she turned with a warm smile. 'You must be Saskia—welcome to the *castello*. We're all just so delighted to meet the future Mrs Gunn.'

Saskia froze, but the woman seemed too caught up in the moment to notice.

'For pity's sake, bring the girl inside—she'll be catching her death. Shall I have hot drinks brought to you? The fires have been lit throughout.'

'Lovely, Imelda, thank you,' Malachi agreed. 'We shall be in the library, I think.'

'You have an English housekeeper?'

'I've known Imelda for almost fifteen years now. I bought this place with my first million, and her late husband was the builder who oversaw much of the renovation work.'

'You didn't do it yourself, then?' she teased.

'I did what I could.' Malachi shrugged. 'But I was still working a lot in the UK back then.'

She waited for him to elaborate further, but he didn't, instead ushering her through long crisscrossing corridors until they stepped through a door into what was clearly the library.

Old leather-bound tomes upon old leather-bound tomes lay behind pretty wrought-iron-framed doors. Wall-to-wall and floor-to-ceiling, save for the gargantuan stone fireplace with its timber mantelshelf which took up a third of one wall, and the two leaded windows, complete with deep sides and cushioned window seats, which nestled into the other.

As they stood in silence, the only noise was the welcoming crackle of the fire as the shadows began to dance around the room. It was only too easy for Saskia to imagine whiling away the rest of her pregnancy here.

He ushered her into the room, taking such tender care of her, before crossing the floor to throw himself into a generous wingback chair, whilst she weighed up the merits of the rest of the seating.

The window seats would afford her a good view, but the wingback chair that matched Malachi's was closer to that inviting fire. So she made her way over and there they sat, in companionable silence, until Imelda brought their drinks, along with some homemade biscuits, still warm from the oven. The older woman fussed over her, ensuring she was comfortable and pain-free, all the while bossing Malachi about and making certain that he was taking care of Saskia.

'She treats you more like a son than an employer,' Saskia said, smiling, when Imelda left the room at last, finally satisfied that her new patient was as comfortable as she could possibly be.

'In many ways she's the mother I never had,' Malachi answered—then stopped sharply, as though he hadn't intended to say anything at all.

'She obviously cares about you a great deal,' she ventured, then waited, hoping that he would say more.

Her heart flip-flopped madly. She knew he had set up the Care to Play charity because she'd met him at the ball, and judging by his close relationship with families like Izzy and Michelle she knew he was more than just financially invested. But Malachi, like his brother, Sol, was such a closed book that those few details were the sum of her knowledge.

It was all Saskia could do not to fall on this new scrap of information as if it was an oasis in the desert and she was a dying woman. But inside she was aching to know more. To understand what made Malachi who he was. To learn what drove him on.

Clearly he didn't intend to elaborate, and she tried not to feel hurt that, even after everything they'd been through with their own little miracle, he still didn't trust her enough to want to open up to her.

It ought to be the wake-up call she needed to remember to keep her guard up where Malachi Gunn was concerned. It was futile to keep wanting—imagining—more with him. In his eyes, their agreement was nothing more than the extension of a business agreement.

She forced herself to take a mouthful of the delicious biscuit. Then another. Anything but give in to the temptation to ask him more about himself and risk him shutting down on her.

But eventually the silence got to her. 'How long are you going to stay?' Saskia spoke at last, when they were alone again.

Really, after Imelda's comments about *the*

Gripping the handrail, Saskia stopped in a glass hallway and fought to draw a breath. She'd thought she didn't know what she wanted. Apparently she knew more than she'd realised.

She wanted her baby to have its father.

Not necessarily marriage, as Malachi had put forward, but...*something*. She'd been lying when she'd told him she could do it alone. Lying to him or to herself, she couldn't be sure. Either way, she should have bent a little more. She should have compromised.

But then she'd never been very good at that. It had been one of the many criticisms that Andy had levelled at her which he'd been right about. Of course there was also an argument to say that if Andy had been a fairer, more honest, more loyal fiancé, then perhaps she would have actually *wanted* to compromise more.

Well, it was too late now. She'd made her bed, as they said. Now she had to go and get scanned on it.

Maybe afterwards, if she was feeling brave, she would take a detour past Malachi's apartment. Perhaps even apologise for her curtness last week.

Lifting her head, Saskia focused on moving forward, one step at a time, until she finally reached the end of the corridor and went through the double doors to the booking-in desk.

* * *

'Cutting it a bit fine, aren't you?'

His dry voice in her ear had Saskia spinning in an instant.

'You came!'

She actually seemed pleased to see him there, and for a moment Malachi was thrown.

He'd half expected her to tell him he was not wanted at the scan. He'd even been prepared for it.

Saskia had laid her position out all too clearly the other night, when she'd turned down his marriage proposal without even a hint of a qualm. She didn't need him and she didn't really even want him—at least not outside the bedroom.

But he was the father of her unborn baby, and he had no intention of letting the child grow up thinking he didn't want to be a part of its life. That he didn't care.

He'd gone through the whole gamut of emotions after Saskia had left his apartment a week ago, yet he still didn't know exactly how he felt. He only knew that he was this baby's father and as such he had a responsibility both to it and to Saskia. Whatever she might wish.

And now she was smiling at him as though she was glad he was here. As though she hadn't told him that she could do it alone. As though she hadn't spelled out that he was nothing more than a rebound to her, and that it made no difference to her whether he was part of their lives or not. As though she hadn't turned on him, dismissing his relevance in her life the way his mother had done to him—and to Sol—all those years ago.

He'd let his guard down with Saskia.

He wouldn't make that mistake again.

'Don't worry. I'm only here for the baby—not for you,' he murmured, as he accompanied her to the chairs, carrying her file in his hand.

She blinked at him, and something he couldn't identify flashed through those rich chocolate depths. Then it was gone.

'Glad to hear it. I wouldn't want to have to turn down yet another hollow marriage proposal.'

'Trust me, I have no intention of repeating that.'

There had to be something wrong with him, because every single word burned in his throat, acrid and bitter, whilst Saskia offered him a curt bob of the head as though finally—barely—she was satisfied.

Malachi gritted his teeth and waited for her name to be called, unable to stop himself from placing his hand at the small of her back as they walked in, helpless to control this protective instinct that surged inside him when he looked at her.

It made no sense. He'd vowed to himself long ago that a wife, children, weren't for him. Hadn't he sacrificed so much of his childhood to playing the part of a parent? It was why he'd set up Care to Play with his brother. In order to help young carers have some semblance of a childhood in a way that he had never enjoyed. But he never wanted to bear that responsibility himself again.

And yet here he was. In a consultation room with a woman who was little more than a stranger and an unborn baby he would never have chosen to have.

But it was what it was, and he would deal with it the best way he could. The way he dealt with everything in his life…

Malachi didn't know the exact moment he went from detached to awestruck.

Perhaps it was when he saw the image come into focus on the sonographer's screen. Or when he saw the distinct outline of the baby's head. Or maybe it was when he heard the strong, rapid beat of his baby's heart.

He didn't know. And yet in that instant everything…*shifted*. His world began to tilt, slowly at first, then faster. It started to rotate, and spin, and he felt himself toppling, then falling.

His baby.

And Saskia's.

And he knew he would go to the ends of the earth to protect it.

'We should talk…' Saskia bit her lip as they stepped out of the consultation room together.